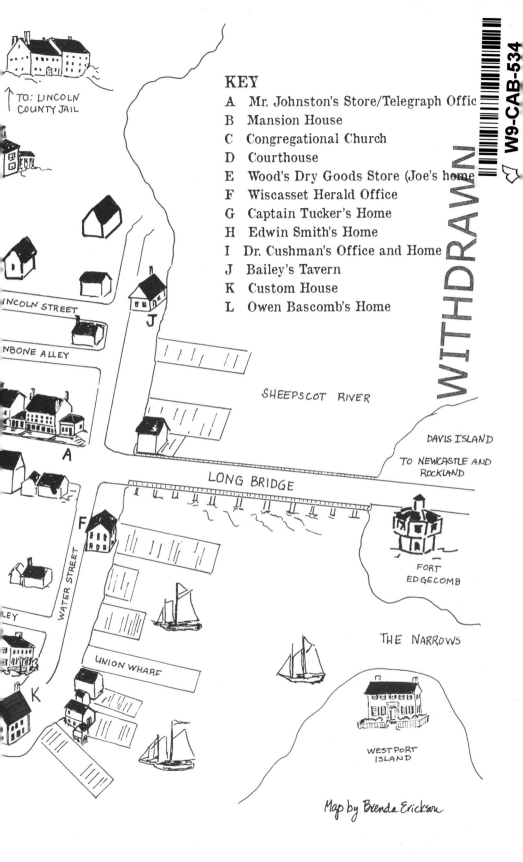

KEY

A Mr. Johnston's Store/Telegraph Office

B Mansion House

C Congregational Church

D Courthouse

E Wood's Dry Goods Store (Joe's home)

F Wiscasset Herald Office

G Captain Tucker's Home

H Edwin Smith's Home

I Dr. Cushman's Office and Home

J Bailey's Tavern

K Custom House

L Owen Bascomb's Home

TO: LINCOLN COUNTY JAIL

LINCOLN STREET

NBONE ALLEY

SHEEPSCOT RIVER

DAVIS ISLAND

TO NEWCASTLE AND ROCKLAND

LONG BRIDGE

WATER STREET

FORT EDGECOMB

THE NARROWS

UNION WHARF

WESTPORT ISLAND

Map by Brenda Erickson

Praise for *Uncertain Glory*

"I was hooked by this suspenseful and moving story of a fourteen-year-old newsman struggling to publish a newspaper in the first days of the Civil War. Lea Wait's lucid writing and beautifully imagined, deftly plotted tale make 19th century Maine as fresh and vivid as today's headlines."
—Maryrose Wood, author of *The Incorrigible Children of Ashton Place* series

"Inspired by the true stories of several remarkable teens, *Uncertain Glory* transports readers to Wicasset, Maine, just as the Civil War begins. The time and place are beautifully evoked, the characters are complex and appealing, and intriguing plot lines and themes are deftly woven together. *Uncertain Glory* is a vivid reminder that even far from the battlefields, the Civil War changed the lives of children, women, and men forever."
—*American Girl* author Kathleen Ernst

"*Uncertain Glory* by Lea Wait is the perfect Civil War novel for young adults, so rich with authentic period details and attitudes that the reader feels transported to Wiscasset, Maine, of 1861. Crosscurrents of patriotism, racism, slavery, and spiritualism rend the town and fourteen-year-old Joe Wood, editor of the local newspaper, is at the center of it all fighting to keep his business afloat. This page-turner juggles complex characters and plot twists to leave readers breathless and challenged to draw their own conclusions about a range of ethical issues."
—Kathleen V. Kudlinski, author of forty children's books including *Facing West*; *A Story of the Oregon Trail* and *Harriet Tubman, Freedom's Trailblazer*

UNCERTAIN GLORY

Other young adult titles from Islandport Press:

Billy Boy: The Sunday Soldier of the 17th Maine
by Jean Flahive

Cooper and Packrat: Mystery on Pine Lake
by Tamra Wight

Mercy: The Last New England Vampire
by Sarah L. Thomson

UNCERTAIN GLORY

by
Lea Wait

ISLANDPORT PRESS

ISLANDPORT PRESS
PO Box 10
Yarmouth, Maine 04096
www.islandportpress.com
books@islandportpress.com

ISBN: 978-1-939017-25-3
Library of Congress Control Number: 2013955829

Book jacket design: Karen Hoots / Hoots Design
Book design: Michelle Lunt / Islandport Press

Since my first book for young people was published, I've had the privilege and joy of visiting with enthusiastic students and dedicated teachers, librarians, and parents throughout the country. This book is for all of them, with thanks for the welcome they've given me and my books.

And for Tori, Vanessa, Taylor, Samantha, Drew, AJ, Henry, Maddy, and their parents, whose lives inspire me every day.

And, always, for my husband, Bob Thomas, who makes my life an adventure and a delight.

"The uncertain glory of an April day . . . "

—William Shakespeare,

Two Gentlemen of Verona (Act I, Scene 3)

Chapter 1

Reverend Merrill, up to the Congregational Church, says God has our lives all planned out for us. And I'll tell you: I'm just Joe Wood, from a little town in Maine. I figger I'm not exactly in a position to question what God has in mind. But between you and me, sometimes those plans of his are pretty hard to make sense of.

Maybe some folks' lives are laid out in nice, straight lines, as easy to see as the trunk of a white mast pine stretching to Heaven. But this rainy April day I felt as though Ma's kittens had grabbed the yarn of my future and left a mess of tangles too knotted to unravel.

Since I can first remember, schoolmasters I've encountered have told me I had a gift for words. I knew from the first I wanted to write 'em down for others to read. Then I learned my numbers helping Ma do accounts at our family's dry goods store. By the time I was old enough to have some sense of the world, it was clear the newspaper business was my destiny. And such was my luck that last year, just four months before my fourteenth birthday, a cousin I hardly knew died and left me a press, and some fonts and rollers and composing sticks. I had all I needed to begin living that future.

I'd already left school, figgering I'd learned pretty much everything a classroom had to teach me. No one was required to attend school, and, after all, classes were seldom full on the best of days. Farmers often kept their sons and daughters home to prepare fields for planting, or help with birthing sheep or cows, or harvest crops.

But I could tell from the first that publishing a newspaper would be more than I could manage on my own. Too many operations called for at least two sets of hands. So I asked my friend Charlie Farrar to help me.

Charlie's more talk than walk, and has few plans that involve tomorrow, but he's got enough energy for ten. He said newspapering might be exciting, so he was with me. I borrowed $65 from Mr. Shuttersworth at the newspaper over to Bath so I could buy paper and some newer fonts. Shuttersworth gave me six months to pay him back, which at the time I thought fair.

Since then I've worked harder than I thought a person could, aside from those who build ships or farm, jobs neither my body nor my mind ever aspired to do. As a result, without too much bragging, the *Wiscasset Herald*'s doing better than most folks expected. I might be the youngest newspaper publisher in Maine—maybe even in all of these United States!—but I have ninety-eight subscribers, with another twenty-five or so copies selling down at Mr. Johnston's store each week. I've also printed a few jobs for local businesses.

Trouble is, I've only managed to save up $42.27 of that $65.00 I owe Mr. Shuttersworth. I've had to keep buying paper, and I needed headline fonts, and it was incumbent upon me to pay both Charlie and Owen Bascomb, who's an apprentice of sorts to me, a few cents on occasion for their help.

If I don't get that last $22.73 by April 22, thirteen days from now, Mr. Shuttersworth is determined he'll take my press and all my printing gear in payment. And that will be the end of the *Wiscasset Herald*. And my future.

Which explains why my mind's filled with dismal thoughts on this dank April day. I've figgered the numbers every which way I can, but getting those extra dollars seems well-nigh impossible.

The job I was doing now would help, though, so I was pushing as hard as I could to get it finished on time, when the door of my printing shop banged open.

"Where've you been?" I said, turning from the type tray I was filling as Charlie rushed in, slamming the door and leaving muddy footprints on the floor. "Without your help it's taken me nearly three hours to set this type. You promised to be here two hours ago!"

"Godfrey mighty! Keep your shirt buttoned! I'm here now."

Charlie's a year and a half older than me, but a foot taller, and sprouting in all directions. He shook off the winter jacket he'd already outgrown and dropped it and his hat on top of the mud he'd tramped in.

"I've been down at the telegraph office, waiting for the latest news to come in. You can't wait until Saturday to get the next edition out. If we set a page with what I just heard, we can sell it door-to-door. Tonight!"

"I have to finish this broadside for Horace Allen," I pointed out. "He's already paid me to get it printed and handed out today."

"You're not listening! The Southern states stopped all supplies going to Fort Sumter, our fort in Charleston Harbor, down in South Carolina. President Lincoln said he'll send supplies to the soldiers there peaceably if he can—but forcibly if he must!"

"Stopping supplies was yesterday's news." I set the last piece of type for the broadside in place. Charlie would think the sky was falling if a squirrel dropped a nut on his head.

In case you hadn't heard, our country's been in a considerable mess since Mr. Lincoln was elected president last year. Seven states have off and left the Union and declared themselves to be what they call the Confederate States of America.

In his speech on becoming president, Mr. Lincoln said he would "hold, occupy and possess" the two federal properties within those Southern states, Fort Pickens in Florida and Fort Sumter in South Carolina. But that holding and occupying is getting harder and more complicated every day.

Charlie grabbed my shoulders roughly and turned me so my face was staring at his chest. "Listen! This morning General Beauregard, head of the Confederate troops in Charleston, demanded that Fort Sumter surrender."

"Whoa!" I pushed Charlie back a pace. "Simmer down! President Lincoln won't let our soldiers surrender to those traitors."

"Exactly," Charlie agreed. "And if neither side backs down . . . we'll be at war!"

That stopped me, I'll fully admit. "How can we be at war with ourselves? The world's gone plumb crazy."

"It may sound crazy to us in Maine, but those seven states that say they're no longer part of the United States are determined. Down at the telegraph office, Captain Richard Tucker, who makes his money shipping cotton from Charleston to England, is pacing the floor right now. He keeps muttering that he's ruined, and only God knows what the future of our country is."

"Captain Tucker's saying that?" Captain Tucker was not only the richest man in town, he was also the calmest. The one folks went to when they needed business help or advice.

"I saw Owen on the street," Charlie said, rolling up his shirtsleeves. "I told him you could use his help. He'll be here as soon as he takes Gilt-head, that blasted parrot of his, home. He even had it out in the rain. I'll set the type for a special edition of the *Herald* about what's happening down in Charleston. You print the broadside. If nothing else happens down south in the next few hours, we can sell the special edition and give out the advertising handbill at the same time."

"I've never set type and printed two sheets in one day," I said.

Of course, if we *could* do that, I'd make more money toward what I owed Mr. Shuttersworth. And, truthfully, when Charlie was here, we could do twice what I could alone.

"We're newspapermen. This is what we do." Charlie grinned. He tossed an empty composing tray onto the table and reached for a case of type fonts. "Finally, something exciting is happening in this town!"

I could use all the help I could get. If Charlie wanted to be a newsman today, that was fine with me.

How many cents could I charge for a one-page bulletin?

And what would happen in the South tomorrow?

Chapter 2

With my oversight Charlie'd written up the Fort Sumter story and now was focused on setting it. Typesetting's intricate work. You have to find every letter and place it, backward, in the composing stick to produce a tray of type you can print.

I was going to operate the press.

First I hung rope lines across the room, low enough so nine-year-old Owen could reach them. He was growing fast, but he wasn't as tall as Charlie or me.

"Thanks, Joe!" Owen said. "Now I won't have to stand on a chair to hang the broadsides to dry."

"Don't knock against any of the papers when you're racing about the room, taking the damp ones from the press to the line," cautioned Charlie.

"I'll be careful," promised Owen, his dark eyes shining. "I won't smudge even one!"

"I know you won't," I told him, patting him on the back. "We'd be up a tree for sure without you, Owen." Even though I couldn't pay the boy much, he sure did work hard.

Once I'd overheard Owen bragging to another boy that he was apprenticed to me. That made me grin. Most boys my age were apprentices themselves. But Owen's family didn't mind his taking time from schooling to be at the *Herald*'s office. He was bright, and I suspect caught

up quickly when he did go to class. His was one of the few families in
town whose forebears had come from Africa, not Europe. It made no
difference to me where someone's family came from. But I wondered
sometimes if it made a difference to others. Owen seemed to have few
friends his own age.

If I lost the press, how would I tell Owen his job had disappeared? I
pushed that thought to the back of my mind.

I rolled ink over the type, placed a sheet of paper over the form,
pulled the heavy lever down on the press, raised it, checked the result-
ing page, pulled the broadside off, and handed it to Owen.

"Today we have to be 'specially quick. We've got to print eighty
copies of this, and at least another eighty of the sheet Charlie's setting
type for now."

Owen held the paper by its edges and read it out loud:

Circular,
ATTENTION,
RESIDENTS OF WISCASSET!

Saturday, April 13, at 7 p.m.
FAMED SPIRITUALIST & ADVISOR
to Respected Gentlemen & Ladies
throughout North America

Miss Nell Gramercy
Will be available to contact Spirits
and reveal the future
in the ballroom of the Mansion House

TICKETS ONLY 25 CENTS!
Available at Mansion House & Pinkham's Stationery Store

"Who's Miss Nell Gramercy?" asked Owen.

"The *Boston Transcript* said she's one of the few spiritualists innocent and pure enough to contact the dead," I told him. "All I can vouch for is she's an orphan, twelve years old, and traveling with her aunt and uncle. Mr. Allen, her uncle, hired me to print these and hand them out around town."

"Can she really talk to dead people?" asked Owen as he carefully hung the sheet over the line. "Could she talk to Caleb?"

Owen's brother Caleb had died of fever a few years back. Owen was only five then, and Caleb four, but he remembered.

"I don't know, Owen," I told him. "I guess some people think she could."

"I'd like to talk to Caleb. I'd ask him what Heaven's like."

Charlie looked over at me and shrugged. I could tell he might have some doubts about Heaven, and he definitely had doubts about Miss Nell Gramercy. But he held his tongue. For Charlie, that was unusual.

"With the possibility of fighting in the South, I wonder if Mr. Allen's thought of canceling her appearance Saturday night," I said, thinking out loud.

"Not a chance," Charlie said. I'd known he couldn't keep his thoughts to himself for long. "People are nervous. They're afraid there'll be war. They'll be looking for answers anywhere they can get them. I'm no spiritualist, but I predict Miss Nell Gramercy will have a ballroom full of people asking her questions Saturday night."

WISGASSET HERALD

POST OFFICE BUILDING, SECOND STORY,
WATER STREET, WISCASSET, ME.

CONFEDERATES DEMAND SUMTER SURRENDER

TODAY, Jefferson Davis, president of the seven states calling themselves the Confederate States of America, ordered Brigadier General P. G. T. Beauregard to demand the surrender of Fort Sumter, the United States fort located on an island in Charleston Harbor, close to that South Carolina city.

Major Robert Anderson, officer in charge of Fort Sumter, has been awaiting the arrival of provisions from the North for his soldiers. On April 6, President Abraham Lincoln ordered a relief expedition from Norfolk, Virginia, to deliver such supplies as were necessary to maintain the occupation of the Fort.

Our president stated publicly and to the governor of South Carolina that these supplies would be "provisions only; and that, if such attempt be not resisted, no effort to throw in men, arms, or ammunition will be made without further notice, or in case of an attack upon the Fort."

THE SUPPLIES HAVE NOT YET ARRIVED

Tension is high at Fort Sumter, as soldiers on both sides await further orders.

Chapter 3

The rain had long since stopped and the sun had set by the time I headed for home.

I'd posted the notice of Saturday's meeting at Stacy's Corner, and then taken the bulletins from house to house on the south side of Main Street. I charged 1 cent for the page of news and handed the announcement of Nell Gramercy's meeting out for free.

Charlie'd been right. People were eager to read the latest word from the South. At least 30 cents were jingling in my pocket that hadn't been there this morning. If Charlie'd sold as many pages on the north side of town, I'd had a very good day indeed.

I'd have to check my paper supply in the morning. If this mess down south continued, more special bulletins might be needed. That would mean more money coming in. More money toward those dollars I owed Mr. Shuttersworth.

My mind was filled with dollars and cents, but my back ached from raising and lowering the devil's tail, the lever that pressed the paper and the tray of type together, and my feet were colder than frost on an iron gate.

Back in February I'd coated my boots with tallow from melted candles to keep out dampness. Tallow helped in winter, when streets were covered with snow and ice. But now we were plumb into mud season. My boots slurped as I walked through the street flooded with melted snow. The morning's rain had made it worse. Cold water seeped in through tiny cracks in the tallow and covered my toes.

I walked faster, thinking how good it'd be to stretch those toes out by the kitchen stove.

My family lives behind and above our store. Now it's only Ma and Pa and me. Since my older brother Ethan drowned Ma's depended on me to help run the store. I help her unpack new fabrics and spools of thread and hats, or assist customers while she does the accounts, or orders new quilted petticoats or deerskin gloves or bolts of velvet.

I don't mind having to take on Ethan's share. But it's been more than that, too. After Ethan died, Pa changed. He hardly ever worked in the store or went to church or even talked with his friends. What he did I couldn't tell you, except he slept a lot, and took long walks by himself into the countryside. Whatever he was doing, he sure wasn't much help to Ma or me.

Ma hasn't complained, but it's been hard on her since I've had the *Herald,* even though I've tried to be at the store when she needed me.

I was thinking just that as I walked into our dooryard. Then it hit me: Today Ma had been expecting a big shipment of spring fabrics in on the Portland stage. She'd asked me to help her get those heavy bolts of fabric to the store.

I hadn't been there.

I felt lower than the smallest spring peeper singing his heart out somewhere down on Water Street. I'd been thinking so much about printing the handbill, and then putting out the special bulletin, that I'd fully forgotten Ma's shipment.

I splashed through deep puddles in our yard and picked up an arm-load of small logs from our woodpile. It'd been a long, cold winter, and the pile was low. In May we'd buy newly cut wood from Mr. Grayson, a lumberman Pa knew, and I'd begin splitting it for next winter.

I pushed open the kitchen door and dumped the wood in the box next to our iron cookstove, trying not to trip over Trusty, my happy nuisance of a small brown-and-white dog. He's been with me four years now, and doesn't understand why he can't go to the *Herald* office. He wriggled all over in excitement at seeing me.

"Good boy," I said, scratching the little spot right behind his left ear, where he loves to be rubbed. "Sorry I couldn't take you with me today. You would have just been in the way with all those papers flying around."

Ma and Pa had already gone to bed. A lantern was burning low on the kitchen table, and salt cod with pork gravy for my supper was in an iron pot on the stove.

I pulled off my wet boots, put copies of the news flyer and the advertisement about Nell Gramercy's meeting on the table for Ma and Pa to read in the morning, and filled my stomach.

What was happening now at that fort down in Charleston Harbor? South Carolina seemed far away. The country might have troubles, but for me, in Wiscasset, Maine, it'd been a good day. Coins were filling my pocket.

A good day except I'd forgotten Ma.

I determined to unpack the new merchandise for the store before I collapsed into bed.

Was anyone sleeping tonight down at Fort Sumter?

Chapter 4

Wednesday, April 10, morning

Charlie's father manages the Mansion House, the grandest inn in Wiscasset. He and his father live there, too, in small rooms on the first floor. Charlie's never talked about having a mother, but by all odds of nature I assume he had one once. Before last July, when he and his father arrived in Wiscasset, they'd lived wherever an inn or small hotel needed managing. Charlie calls Wiscasset "the most boring town in the world." He's never been real clear as to where those other places he lived were, but I have a suspicion none of them were up to his standards either.

On Wiscasset's side, Charlie does grudgingly admit that Mrs. Giles, the Mansion House cook, is one of the best he's ever encountered in her profession. He turns on whatever charm he can manage when she's about. As a result, he's pretty well-fed, and as his friend, I sometimes benefit.

That Wednesday morning he'd wheedled a half-dozen rolls out of her, two of which he tossed to me. I caught them before they joined the dried mud and scraps of paper left on the office floor the day before. Ma makes good bread, but not the soft white rolls they serve at the Mansion House. The rolls were still warm. I took a generous bite.

"I stopped at the telegraph office. Only news is that some actor named John Wilkes Booth is performing *Richard III* in Portland tomorrow night, and he's announced he'll include a patriotic tribute to the soldiers at Fort Sumter. Telegraphic dispatch said Portland folks are lining up for tickets," Charlie said.

I shook my head. "Nothing important enough for an extra edition. Nobody from Wiscasset's going to go fifty miles to see a play. Even *with* a patriotic tribute. How much money'd you take in last night?"

"Twenty-nine cents. You?"

"Thirty-two." I pointed to the coins on the corner of the desk.

"Your part of town had more houses. But I got some of the men in the tavern and at the inn to buy sheets." Charlie added his coins to mine. "Not a bad day's work."

"Especially since I'd already been paid four dollars in cash to print and deliver the broadside," I agreed. "Too bad rich city folks don't come here every week to pay for their printing." I opened my ledger to check the tally. Sixty-one more cents in the plus column meant I had $42.88. Every cent counted, but I still had a long ways to go. I'd already figgered in the $4 from Mr. Allen.

"I saw your Mr. Allen at the inn this morning," said Charlie. "He's pleased with the broadside. People are already asking that Miss Gramercy conduct a smaller, more private, session—one that's open to folks who can afford to pay more than twenty-five cents."

"Is she going to do it?" At 25 cents a ticket, how much money were Miss Gramercy and her uncle going to make? Sounded like the spiritualism business sure was an easier way to make a living than the newspaper business.

"Father's trying to set it up for tomorrow evening. Mr. Allen's insisting on having a special room, arranged a certain way."

"So, what do you think? Can that girl really talk with the dead?"

"Nah . . . how could she?" Charlie started taking the fonts we used yesterday out of the chase so we could clean and file them.

"Lots of famous people believe in spiritualists. I read in the *Boston Transcript* that President Lincoln's wife consults them. She even invited one to dine at the White House," I pointed out.

"The *Transcript* said that this Nell Gramercy was one of the best," Charlie acknowledged. "It said no one had been able to prove she wasn't honest." He suddenly slammed his fist down on the printers' table, bouncing the trays of fonts. "That's it! That's it, Joe!"

"That's what?" I was used to Charlie going off in all directions at once. Soon enough he'd tell me what bee was in his bonnet this time.

"We're newsmen, right? This is a story! You don't want to run a little four-page weekly in Wiscasset, Maine, all your life! Here's our chance to show the world we can be serious journalists. If we can prove the famous Nell Gramercy is a fraud and is getting good Maine people to pay her money to invent stories, our article will be picked up by other newspapers. Editors will recognize our names when we look for jobs at bigger papers, in bigger cities."

Charlie walked to the window and put his hand on the cold glass. "Wiscasset is fine for now, but I want to write stories that are important. To do that, you have to be where exciting things happen. In Boston, or New York. Or Washington!"

He turned back toward me, his voice rising with excitement. "A newspaperman can do anything if he has enough respect. Hannibal Hamlin, President Lincoln's vice president, started as a newspaperman right here in Maine."

"As I recall he stopped off between the newspaper business and Washington to study lawyering," I reminded Charlie. "Wiscasset is plenty exciting enough for me." I rescued the fonts that had ended up on the floor when Charlie'd hit the table. "People know each other here, and care what happens to their neighbors. Besides, what if Nell Gramercy *is* talking with the dead? What if it isn't a trick?"

"People who're dead are dead. Forever. Gone. Somehow she's fooling people. I'm going to find a way for us to go to that session her uncle's setting up for tomorrow night, Joe. Once we see what she's doing, then we can tell whether she's honest or not."

"I have enough to do, keeping up with news from the South, and putting out the regular issue of the *Herald* on Saturday."

"I'll stop at the telegraph office, then I'll go to the inn. I'll find a way for us to see this Nell Gramercy ourselves."

The door slammed shut. Charlie was gone as quickly as he'd arrived.

The trays of type we'd printed from yesterday still had to be taken apart, cleaned, and the fonts re-filed. The floor needed to be swept.

Working with Charlie was exciting. He always seemed to be all fired up about something. And he was a help. But truth was, he did vanish whenever there wasn't fun or excitement involved.

Did I really want to fool with someone who could talk with the dead?

Charlie was right about sales, though. An article on the Gramercy girl might sell copies—and more copies meant more money.

I picked up the broom and started preparing the office for whatever would come next.

I had a feeling I wouldn't have long to wait.

Chapter 5

Thursday, April 11, evening

"Move over! Your knee's jabbin' my back." I tried to stretch without moving the cloth covering the table Charlie and I were hiding under. My shoulders were cramping. "Real reporters wouldn't do this! We've been here an hour, and nothing's happened. We can't write an article about nothing."

I'd fed Trusty before I left home, but I hadn't eaten supper myself. My belly was aching. Instead of eating Ma's beef and dumplings, I was curled up under a table in the parlor of the most elegant hotel in Wiscasset, listening to my stomach growl. No doubt everyone else at the Mansion House was savoring oyster stew or chicken with gravy and biscuits in the dining room.

"We're newsmen on a story," said Charlie. "We're tough. We don't have to be comfortable." He was clearly enjoying himself. "While we wait we can set the scene. Listen." He began to whisper what he'd already scribbled in his notebook: *"The parlor at the old Mansion House was dark, lit only by seven whale oil lamps, their flickering light reflected in old-fashioned mirrored wall sconces. A round table and eight chairs were set in the center of the large room, waiting for whatever was to come."*

A gust of wind rattled the shutters and swayed the heavy velvet draperies covering the windows.

"Outside, spring winds howled," Charlie continued, wiping his pen on his already-ink-stained waistcoat. "The editor of the *New York Tribune* or

Boston Transcript will have to be impressed. How can anyone refuse to hire us after they read this?"

"Shouldn't the session have started by now?" I asked.

When Charlie was excited he forgot everything else—including food. Besides, if Charlie smiled sweetly, Mrs. Giles would ensure he didn't starve, even if he appeared in the inn kitchen after the supper hour. I hoped Ma'd left something for me to eat. This would be the second day in a row I'd missed a meal. She wouldn't think kindly of that.

The clock over the marble fireplace chimed the quarter-hour.

"It's almost eight," I pointed out. "Shouldn't people be here by now?"

"All day, people who haven't been talking about South Carolina have been talking about Nell Gramercy. Father said folks have been asking for her uncle, trying to reserve a seat for tonight's spirit reading. Everyone wants to be among the first to hear her." Charlie smiled knowingly. "And we'll be able to see how she tricks them."

I'll admit, the whole situation was making me nervous. And it wasn't just the hiding under a table. Communicating with dead people might sound exciting when you're sitting comfortably in a safe place, like the print shop office. But in this dark room, with the wind banging against the windowpanes like a wild creature trying to get in, I was beginning to question the whole idea of being here at all.

Charlie tried to stretch the arm he was leaning on. "Anyone who says they can hear the dead talk is crazy, or just out to make money. Or both. Mr. Allen's charging a whole dollar to attend this session. A dollar could pay for a whole year's subscription to the *Herald*."

He didn't need to tell me that.

Finally, one after another, six people entered the room and silently took their places at the table. We took turns peeking through a small hole in the red embroidered tablecloth to see who they were.

Captain Tucker and his wife lived up on High Street and were the wealthiest people in town. Old Mrs. Quinn and her daughter, Miss Rachel Quinn, were both dressmakers and midwives. Mrs. Dana was the wife of Wiscasset's leading pharmacist.

But the biggest surprise was the last person to enter the room. Charlie grabbed my arm, and I stifled a gasp as my own pa, Abiel Wood, joined the other five.

The six smiled self-consciously at each other in the light of the flickering lamps. None of them suspected we were spying on them from under a table in the far corner of the dark room.

Mr. Allen, a tall man wearing elegant gray trousers and a long frock coat with an embroidered waistcoat, entered through a door on the other side of the room. He bowed to those already seated.

He cleared his throat. "In these particularly difficult days for our country, when our hearts are torn asunder by our concerns for the future of our beloved nation, you in Wiscasset are especially fortunate to have in your midst the renowned spiritualist, Miss Nell Gramercy. The wealthy and powerful have sought out Miss Gramercy's services, but this evening her special talents are yours. Please understand that using the rare abilities she possesses puts an enormous strain on the nervous system of one so young and innocent, so tonight our spirit circle will last only so long as her strength will allow."

As he finished speaking, the door in back of him opened.

Uncertain Glory

All the gentlemen at the table rose as Nell Gramercy entered the room. She was small for twelve, and dressed entirely in white. Her pale blonde hair was worn down, tied with a piece of white lace at the back of her neck, as was appropriate for her age, although her hooped skirts reached the floor. No Wiscasset girl wore her skirts that long until she was at least sixteen.

I couldn't keep my eyes off the hole in the tablecloth, but Charlie jostled me so he could look, too. Nell's dress and fair hair reflected the dim lamplight, giving her a ghostlike glow in the dark room.

"I'm honored you have all come to welcome me, a stranger to your town. Please be seated." The men took their seats. She nodded at her uncle, who placed a cushion for her on the chair closest to a wall sconce, and took the chair next to hers. Even seated on the pillow, Nell Gramercy was tiny next to the adults.

But her firm, soft voice demanded attention. "Before we begin, I must warn you that I have no control over what might happen tonight. The spirits choose when they communicate, and with whom. No doubt you are all hoping for messages from loved ones lost to you, but not all those souls may wish to join us tonight. Do not be frightened by any noises or vibrations or movements within this room. The spirits have many ways of communicating. I cannot predict their actions."

She raised her thin arms above the round mahogany table, and then lowered them, slowly, reaching out to Mrs. Dana and her uncle, who were seated on either side of her. "Let us join our hands in a circle, so the departed know it is safe to come to us. First, we will have a moment of silence, to show respect for those who may choose to reveal themselves tonight."

The men and women clasped each other's hands on top of the table. A chill draft wafted through the room. Light from the lamp wicks dimmed, although no one had touched them.

No one spoke.

My muscles tightened. Everyone was waiting . . . watching for something to happen. We didn't know what.

Mrs. Tucker giggled nervously.

Nell frowned. "For the spirits to join us, they must sense that everyone present believes in their possibilities."

Everyone was silent. Flickering lamplight was the only movement in the room.

Suddenly Nell bent over the table and began to retch. Deep coughs racked her body. She reached deep into her throat and began pulling out strands of a thin white substance, forming a cloud-like pile on the table in front of her. I couldn't take my eyes off her. Finally, the trail of whatever was emerging from her mouth ended. What was that stuff? What was happening?

As the others at the table watched in fascinated horror, she started to mold the pile of—*what?*—with her fingers. The elderly Mrs. Quinn, who attended the Congregational Church every Sunday, clutched a handkerchief to her heart.

"A letter is coming to me," Nell said. Her eyes stared into the distance, like blind Mr. Gould did. "It may be the first letter of a name. It's hazy . . . I'm trying to see . . . I believe it may be an 'N.' " The room was silent. "No—an 'M.' "

Mrs. Quinn gasped. "Michael? Is it you, Michael?"

"Does the letter M mean something to you, then? A spirit has a message for someone in this room," said Nell, turning to the old lady. Then she hesitated, as though listening to something no one else could hear. "But, no—there seem to be two M's . . . perhaps two spirits . . ."

"My dear husband and my boy; both were Michaels," Mrs. Quinn whispered.

"A male spirit, of some years, is with us," continued Nell. Her voice was low and steady, as though she were repeating words she'd heard somewhere else. "He desires his wife to know he is well, and dwells with a much younger spirit. I believe the younger spirit may be your son. Your husband wants you to know he loves you, and will see you again, in Heaven."

Tears dripped down the widow's lined face. "Does he say anything else?"

Nell paused. She then pulled the white substance on the table apart and it fell into dust. "That spirit has now gone from us. Gone, with the ectoplasm. He has nothing more for us today. Perhaps another time." She looked at Mrs. Quinn, who was dabbing her eyes with her handkerchief. "I'm afraid spirits do not often stay with us long. Their sense of time is eternal, unlike ours. But other spirits are waiting. The spirit circle must not be broken."

Mrs. Quinn nodded. She dropped the handkerchief in her lap and reached for the hands of those next to her.

Nell's voice was low. "I now see a harbor, filled with ships."

Charlie grinned and elbowed me. I figgered I knew what was in his mind. Nell could guess pretty easy that someone in this room had a connection to ships. Wiscasset Harbor was filled with ships, even in winter when ice held them captive.

Captain Tucker leaned toward the girl. Three generations of Tucker men had owned and captained vessels.

"I see a ship, far from home." Nell's voice was now a low moan, hard to separate from the crying wind. "It lies heavy in the waters. I see darkness. Smoke. The heaviness of storm clouds . . ."

"What's her name?" Captain Tucker asked quickly. "Which ship is it? Where?"

Nell hesitated and then shook her head. "That I cannot make out, through the noise of the storm."

"Will the ship or any on it come to harm?" Captain Tucker leaned across the table toward Nell. "Will anyone drown?"

Nell's body swayed from side to side, as though she herself were on board a foundering ship. "I cannot say. The ship has now gone from me." She turned her head slightly, as though listening to a voice from another direction. "But someone has drowned. In another place, another time." She hesitated. "A young spirit. One who has not been long gone from this place."

Was Nell actually hearing spirit voices? Or seeing things that would happen? Could she really know what happened to someone who'd died?

"The young spirit is very anxious. He says I must deliver a message to his father."

Pa stared at Nell. "Is it my Ethan? Can you hear him?"

Nell's eyes were closed, and her body swayed as though moved by invisible winds. "I see deep seas closing. Waters not far from here."

"Yes," Pa whispered.

I had to hold back from reaching out—from letting Pa know I was there, too.

"Your son wants you to know he is well and happy. That his leaving . . . was not your fault." Nell's voice was calm and flat, as though she was reciting the words instead of speaking them. "He took the skiff without permission. It was his foolishness, not your sin. You must no longer dwell in the past. He is at peace, and so must you be."

How could Nell know about Ethan? How could she know that Pa blamed himself for Ethan's boat's leaking and sinking in The Narrows? Only Ma and I knew that Pa had planned to patch the skiff with pitch, but had been helping Ma that day and forgotten.

I shivered. Charlie said we should prove this girl was a fraud. But what if she wasn't? What if she *could* talk with dead people? How else could she have known about Ethan?

Chapter 6

We waited 'til everyone had left the parlor before making our escape down a back stairway to the kitchen. I didn't complain none when Charlie managed to scrounge a platter filled with enough sliced lamb and bread for both of us. Mrs. Giles beamed at our thanks as we hightailed it to his room.

For the first few minutes we didn't talk. Fresh bread and young roasted lamb slathered with mint jelly is worth concentrating on.

Finally I said out loud what I'd been thinking. "Nell Gramercy may truly be communicatin' with spirits. She's only been in Wiscasset a few days. How could she have known Mrs. Quinn's husband and son were both dead, and both named Michael?" I kept my thoughts about Ethan to myself.

Charlie shook his head. "It's all humbug. Has to be. No one can get messages from the dead. She must have found out ahead of time about the people who're coming to her sessions."

"Not if the spirits speak to her directly," I pointed out. "And what about that . . . that white stuff that came out of her mouth?"

"I've read about spiritualists. That stuff she called ectoplasm is supposed to show that spirits have entered the medium's body, or something like that. Sometimes spirits knock, to give answers or spell out words, or move furniture in the room when a spiritualist is working.

Some spiritualists make fog-like figures appear. I would've liked to have seen that! Or the table rising into the air!"

"It was spooky enough to see her cough up that stuff and hear what she was saying," I said. I didn't need ghosts appearing or knocking or furniture floating around. "If we report what we saw, we have to say that Nell Gramercy got messages from dead people."

Charlie shook his head and brushed crumbs off his shirt front onto the floor. "The Boston paper said ectoplasm may be spiderwebs, all mashed up together, that the spiritualist hides in her cheeks."

My stomach turned sideways. I pushed the almost-empty platter of lamb away.

"Maybe it's not true. But no matter what it was, I think she knew what she was going to say before she went in that room."

"But how could she? Unless we know how she got her information, we can't say she *didn't* communicate with spirits."

Charlie crumpled the piece of paper on which he'd taken notes earlier that evening. "I don't know. But you're right—we have to find out more. Nell Gramercy is just a girl. She's younger than we are. She can't be doing all this herself. Maybe that uncle of hers is somehow telling her what to do and say. He sold the tickets. He knew who would be there."

"How could he tell her anything? He hardly spoke tonight."

"He must have a way. Some signal. We just have to figure it out." Charlie turned to me. "What did she say to your father? I didn't even know you had a brother."

"I don't talk about him much," I said. "If you'd been in Wiscasset longer, you'd have known. Ethan was older than me. His skiff was caught in the current at The Narrows, between Westport and Davis Islands. It sank about eighteen months ago."

"I'm sorry. You must miss him a lot." Charlie was silent for a moment. "I always wanted a brother."

"Ethan and I fished together and went sliding on Courthouse Hill in winter. He wanted to be a mariner and sail to the South Seas." I stood up. I didn't feel comfortable talking about Ethan. Charlie didn't know what it was like to lose a brother. "Thank Mrs. Giles for the grub. I've got to get to home. Ma'll be worried."

"I'll come over to the office early tomorrow," Charlie said. "Right after I check the news from the South. I'll help you finish up Saturday's issue and start printing it. With or without a story about Nell Gramercy."

Chapter 7

Friday, April 12, morning

I didn't see Pa or Ma Thursday night. The only one waiting up for me was Trusty, so I didn't know if Pa had told Ma he'd gone to Nell Gramercy's session, and what she'd said. 'Course, he didn't know I was there, so I couldn't have said anything anyway.

I feared I'd blurt out something I shouldn't, so I got up even earlier than usual and headed for the *Herald* office, straightaway. With the paper due out Saturday afternoon, and having spent more than two days on the broadside and the bulletin, I reckoned there was plenty to do in the next twenty-four hours.

"C'mon, Trusty. Today you can come with me to the office." Despite his words last night I knew I couldn't count on Charlie. Trusty would be good company.

The early morning was cool, but the sun was beginning to lighten the sky. Piles of drifted snow remained where shadows of trees and houses kept them from the direct rays of the sun, but the ice was out of the river, finches were chirping mating songs in bushes along the road, and above me Canadian geese honked as they headed north for the summer. An eagle flew downriver. The day was full of April's promise.

Trusty sniffed every horse and ox turd, every stagnant puddle left from the week's rains, and joyfully chased a gray squirrel up a greening tree. He was so happy to be out of the house and yard that I took the long way around, walking down by the shipyards and wharves and then along Water Street. All was peaceful.

Until we reached Main Street.

Despite the hour, a crowd was gathered outside Mr. Johnston's store. Miss Mary Averill, the telegraph operator, worked in an office in back of the counter there. To be truthful, a part of me didn't want to know what the other part understood had happened. But news has got to be faced, especially if you're a newsman. I ran to join the others. Trusty ran with me, barking excitedly at the crowd.

Mr. Colby was holding his wife, who was sobbing. Several knots of men were deep in conversation. Others stood alone. Then I saw Charlie.

"There you are!" Charlie said. "I wanted to get you, but I didn't want to miss any new wires. Miss Averill slept at the store last night so as not to miss any messages, but they didn't start coming in until an hour ago."

"What's happened?"

"Yesterday the Confederate general, Beauregard, ordered Major Anderson at Fort Sumter to surrender and leave the fort. Of course Major Anderson refused. Then, at 4:27 this morning, the Confederate battery at Fort Moultrie fired at Fort Sumter. And Major Anderson's men fired back."

"And then?"

"That's all we know! That's why everyone is standing here. Waiting."

"How long does it take to find out?"

"A telegraph operator in Charleston is sending messages north along the wires to relay stations. I don't know how many stations are between South Carolina and Maine, but messages are sent to Portland,

and then to Yarmouth, Brunswick, and Bath. The Bath office sends them here. The telegraph is an amazing invention, but it can't send messages hundreds of miles at once."

"If the first office is in Charleston, could be that it's only tellin' the Southern side of the story."

"Telegraph officers are said to be honest."

"I suppose." It seemed almost impossible. Here we were, standing on a street in the State of Maine, waiting to hear what a man or woman in a Southern city tapped out in dots and dashes on a telegraph key. "Men could be dying in Charleston right now, and we'll know about it in only three or four hours," I said. "That's never happened in a war before."

"And President Lincoln can go to the telegraph office at the War Department and know what his army is doing," agreed Charlie.

Suddenly I had a selfish thought. More people were joining the crowd on Main Street all the time. Maybe the future of my chosen profession was doomed. Who would buy a newspaper when they could get news within hours from the telegraph? I shared my worries with Charlie.

"Not everyone can stand here all the time," Charlie pointed out. "And what about people still at their homes or farms? They haven't heard what's happening yet. Plus, telegraph wires aren't strung everywhere."

"True. But tomorrow's *Herald* will have to be as up-to-date as possible. With news changing this fast, there's no way to tell what might be happening by the time we deliver the paper."

Trusty followed us as we moved through the crowd.

"I had an idea last night, after you left," said Charlie. "We could interview Nell Gramercy."

"What?" I reached down and stopped Trusty from impolitely sniffing old Mrs. Gould. "Interview Miss Gramercy? Are you crazy? I'm worrying about covering a battle in South Carolina, and you're talking about interviewing a girl spiritualist."

"She's news, too! Local news. And she's going to hold that big meeting tomorrow night no matter what happens down south."

"So?"

"I'll help. We'll fill three pages of the *Herald* with the ads and social notices and fillers you already have. We'll keep checking with the telegraph office until right before we have to set type for page one, tomorrow morning. If anything happens after that, it has to be a special edition, like the one two days ago. You made money on that! On the first page, we'll put an article on the happenings in South Carolina, and what people here think about it. And, if we can get it, an interview with Nell Gramercy."

"Her uncle might think more people would pay to see her after reading it," I admitted.

"Exactly."

"I'll need your help, and Owen's. Full-time," I added.

"You go and get Owen. I'll find Mr. Allen. He's usually in the tavern, even in the morning," Charlie said. "Father sends people there if they want to know anything about the spirit sessions."

"I'll take Trusty home first. Then I'll find Owen. Meet me back at the office," I told him. "When you find out whether we can interview Nell Gramercy, we'll know how many columns we'll have to fill."

Charlie had a talent for getting what he went after. He might just get us that interview with Miss Gramercy.

Chapter 8

Trusty happily trotted back home to Middle Street with me. He didn't know he was going to be left behind the fence that enclosed the dooryard. Keeping Trusty with me if I was going to be at the newspaper office all day by myself was one thing, but I didn't want to worry about him if Charlie, Owen, and I were all going to be in and out of the office, interviewing people, checking with the telegraph office, and racing back to write stories.

Besides, I wanted to tell Ma and Pa the news. They wouldn't know about the battle in Charleston Harbor.

Trusty squeezed his way inside the shop ahead of me. Ma already had a customer. Mrs. Pendleton was trying on one of the spring hats that had arrived by coaster last week from New York City. Ma was helping her decide which color flattered her most. She looked up and nodded at me. "Your father's in the back."

Had Pa told her he'd gone to the spirit circle last night?

A bang echoed from the room in back of the store. I gathered up Trusty, who gave one reluctant bark, and we went through the back door of the shop into the private area of the building. Trusty wasn't normally allowed in the store; that was the territory of Snowball, Ma's large white cat.

Drafts from the cellar windows had been blowing the door from the cold cellar to the kitchen open for weeks now. No doubt the door was

35

banging again. I reminded myself to get new hinges. In the meantime, Ma and I had been piling crates in front of the door. The crates weren't enough to keep the door closed when the wind was from the north, but they should've been enough on this calm, sunny morning.

But, no. The sound I'd heard was the hammer Pa'd dropped. I stared. Pa hadn't fixed anything since Ethan had died. This morning he was screwing new hinges onto the cellar door.

"You're home, son! I heard that darn door knocking against the crates again and decided this would be the day to fix it, so I got some new hinges over to the blacksmith shop on Water Street. Hand me that hammer, would you?"

I did.

"You're awfully quiet. Don't you like the hinges I chose?" Pa pointed. "They're bigger than the ones we had before, and fancy, with the ends swirled and all, but the holes for the smaller ones were too loose. These should hold better, and add a bit of elegance to the room." He hit a hard blow to a nail whose hole would serve for the screw he'd put in next.

"The hinges are fine. Where are the umbrellas and buttons and silk flowers for hats?" The crates and barrels of inventory I hadn't finished unpacking two nights before were gone.

"I sorted those and got them out into the shop. Your mother likes to get the new merchandise on display as quickly as she can, you know. Always says it brightens folks up to think ahead to summer this time of year."

It had been months since Pa had shelved any new items for the store, and he'd only done it then because Ma had nagged him. "Are you feeling all right, Pa?"

"Right as rain. Better, since the sun is finally shining! Just woke up this morning and decided I'd rested long enough. Seemed a good day to make a new start. I'm sorry not to have helped out as much as I should have recently, but I'm proud of all you've done for your ma, especially with the printing business taking so much of your time."

He put a screw in the hinge. "You've been doing a darn good job with the newspaper. I see you've been picking up printing jobs, too. I appreciated your leaving those bulletins for us on the table two nights ago."

"I thought you'd want to know the news when you woke in the morning."

Pa swept up the sawdust.

"There's more news now, Pa. Bad news. The Confederates fired on Fort Sumter down in Charleston Harbor early this morning. We're shootin' back."

Pa stopped sweeping. "Ever since Mr. Lincoln was elected, this country's gone from bad to worse. But he had to take a stand some-where. If he let those cotton states think they could just pack up and start their own country, then what would stop any state from getting its britches in a knot and doing the same? And that would be the end of this United States your great-grandfather fought so hard to create." He shook his head. "I hope the differences are settled soon, Joe. I hate to think what it will mean for all of us if they're not."

"The fighting's just in South Carolina, Pa. The only one in Wiscasset who might be affected is Captain Tucker. He has an office and ships in Charleston, doesn't he?"

"He does. And I pray you're right, Joe. I do."

"In town, no one's doing anything but waiting for news. Charlie and I are going to stay close to Miss Averill at the telegraph office today. We're going to lay out the rest of tomorrow's *Herald,* and leave the front page for tomorrow, to be sure we include the latest news. Maybe the conflict will be settled by then."

"Well, good news or bad, this door had to be fixed, and the world will go on. Would you hold the door so I can fasten the last hinge?"

As the final screw was twisted in, Ma opened the door from the shop. "What a sight! My two men working together, and handsome new hinges on that broken door." She looked around the room. "The kitchen hasn't looked so tidy in weeks."

"I'm sorry, Ma," I said. "I've been so busy with the print shop."

"I know you have; I understand. But still, I'm pleased to have extra help here." Her smile was for Pa. She hadn't smiled like that when I'd done 'most everything for the past year and a half. "Joe, did your father tell you what happened last night?"

Pa had told Ma about the spirit circle. It had to be that. "No. He didn't say anything."

"Joe, I heard from Ethan last night." Pa's voice was proud and excited.

I sat down. I mustn't let them know Charlie and I had been at the Mansion House.

"I went to hear that spiritualist. You left the broadside on the table, or I wouldn't have known about her. She's very young—too young to understand all she's saying, I suspect. But she spoke to Ethan. He said he was well." Pa's smile was the most relaxed it had been since Ethan's body had been found on the mudflats. "It was a miracle, but it happened. That Nell Gramercy heard him."

"Your father's bought tickets for us both to go to her session tomorrow night," added Ma, "and he's arranged for us to have a private session with her next week. If she can get in touch with Ethan, then I want to hear, too."

"It was amazing, son. She knew things about Ethan that only one of us would have known. After I knew he was well, and not angry with me, I slept better last night than I have in months. I don't know how that girl's able to get in touch with those who have passed on, but she does. She brought messages from old Mrs. Quinn's husband and son, too, and told Captain Tucker that one of his ships was in a storm. That 'storm' might have even meant the battle you just told me about!"

"Battle?" asked Ma, turning to me. "What battle?"

"Down in South Carolina. The Confederates fired on Fort Sumter, and the Federal forces fired back. It began early this morning," I explained.

"Just when we were beginning to feel at peace about Ethan," Ma said, sitting down hard on one of the kitchen chairs and reaching for Pa's hand. "Let's pray war won't take our other son from us."

Chapter 9

Friday, April 12, mid-morning

I walked slowly back to the *Herald*'s office. The sun was higher in the sky and the chickadees were still calling to each other, but I focused on kicking pebbles into the deep puddles in the street. They plunked with a satisfying sound.

Political arguments had always seemed boring and far away—something politicians in Washington and businessmen like Captain Tucker worried about. Of course, for years I'd heard people talking about why slavery should be ended. Why, *Uncle Tom's Cabin,* Mrs. Stowe's book that described the evils of slavery, was written in Brunswick, just twenty miles down the road. A person in this town'd have to be deaf, dumb, and blind not to know about abolitionists and their campaign to end slavery in all the states, not just here in the North. Slavery hadn't been allowed in Maine since 1783, way back when we were still part of Massachusetts. Families like Owen's had lived here freely since then.

But now the men at Fort Sumter weren't talking. They were shooting—and being shot at.

I maneuvered my way through the crowd near Mr. Johnston's store. The clock in the window read ten-thirty.

"Are they still fighting down in Charleston?" I asked Mr. Sayward, who was standing near the door.

"Last message in said batteries on both sides been shelling steadily since a little past seven."

"So no one's won," I said.

"Or lost," Mr. Sayward confirmed.

I nodded, and turned back through the crowd.

Charlie was waiting at the print shop.

"Where've you been?" said Charlie. "And where's Owen? You were going to get him."

"I got distracted."

"I've got good news—even though it won't help for this issue. Mr. Allen was at the tavern, as I thought. I gave him a copy of last week's *Herald* and told him we'd like to cover the meeting Saturday night, and interview Miss Gramercy for our next issue."

"And?" I asked.

"He's given us each free tickets—press passes, he called them—for Saturday night. And we're to meet with Miss Gramercy and her aunt at one o'clock on Monday afternoon." Charlie pulled two tickets out of his pocket and waved them in my face.

"Did he give you a ticket for me, too?" asked Owen, who'd just appeared in the doorway.

"Owen! Good. Joe was just about to go and get you. We can use your help today," said Charlie.

"Can I go to the spirit meeting Saturday?" Owen repeated.

"No; the tickets are just for Joe and me," answered Charlie. "We'll be writing the article."

"I'm learning to write, too," said Owen. "I could help." He picked up the broom and started sweeping the floor.

"Not this time, Owen. And Joe, between seeing Miss Gramercy the other night, and Saturday, and then again Monday to ask her questions, she won't be able to keep any secrets from us. After all, she's just a girl."

"A girl who'll have her aunt with her," I pointed out.

"We're lucky it's just her aunt; her uncle had another appointment then. After all, it wouldn't be proper for her to meet with us without a chaperone. Her aunt won't be answering our questions."

Owen knocked the broom against the wall as he put it back in place and stomped over to the font cases, where he'd practiced setting type for a business card last week.

"What if Nell Gramercy doesn't have any secrets?" I asked. "What if she *can* talk to people in the spirit world?"

"That's impossible," said Charlie. "All we have to do is find out how she does it—how she knows what to say to people."

"It may not be that easy." I kept thinking of how excited my parents were to have heard from Ethan. "She was very convincing last night. And not everyone in Wiscasset may want to hear that Nell is fooling them."

"That's next week's problem," Charlie said dismissively. "Today we have to set type for tomorrow's edition."

"Right," I agreed. "Owen, would you like to set a couple of the ads?"

Owen looked up and nodded, grinning. "I can do it, Joe. I can!"

"Then let's get started. I have the social news and some ads already set, but there are empty spots on pages two, three, and four, and we'll have to redo the first page with the news from Charleston. Owen, there are three spaces left to fill with ads on page four. Why don't we finish those first, and then check the telegraph office?" I kept thinking of what Pa and Ma had said about the fighting. "We could talk to people there, and to those at the tavern and the inn, and find out what they think the attack on Fort Sumter means to the country, and to us here in Maine."

"Good plan," said Charlie. "That way we could quote people and put their names in the paper, too. People buy copies of a newspaper when their names are in it."

Owen was already carefully setting the type for an ad for the Mansion House. Charlie and I took trays to work on the other two pages. All was silent as we each reached for the pieces of type we needed.

Owen was the first to speak. "Do you think many soldiers will be killed down at Charleston Harbor?"

"Could be," answered Charlie. "Men die in battles, and what's happening at Fort Sumter sounds like the closest thing to a real battle the United States has been in since the war with Mexico."

"What do you think it would be like to be a soldier?" Owen asked.

Charlie stopped for a moment and gazed off into space. "And fight for the honor of our nation? It would be glorious."

Chapter 10

Friday, April 12, evening

Both sides in Charleston were still firing late that afternoon. Faces at Wiscasset taverns were getting grimmer, but only a few men still waited at the telegraph office. Events were happening more slowly than most had thought. Or hoped.

Meals had to be cooked, oxen shod, boats caulked, babies fed. Life must go on.

Owen and Charlie left the office to get their suppers, but I stayed to complete the week's accounts and ensure supplies for next week's *Herald* and any special editions were in order. Knocking on wood, I figgered I could just make it through the next ten days before Mr. Shuttersworth showed up with his hand out.

I'd said a silent prayer of thanks when Mr. Dana came by in the afternoon to order business cards for his pharmacy. Luckily, I had plenty of the heavier paper the cards required. It'd take a dozen special orders like his to come up with the cash I needed, but every order counted. I'd already started Owen setting type for the cards.

Warm daytime temperatures had fallen sharply. Now thick fog filled the streets. My boots skidded where the morning's puddles had frozen. I was glad to reach home and inhale the welcoming smells of chicken broth and baked bread. It was a minute or so before I realized Trusty hadn't greeted me at the door.

"Trusty?" I called. "Trusty?"

"Trusty's in the yard," Ma called from upstairs. "I was about to bring him in. This dank fog's no weather for even a dog to be out in for long. Thank goodness you're home."

I lit the tin kerosene lantern with the glass front and went outside. "Trusty?" No answering bark. I checked the dooryard fence for openings. Small paw prints were all over the muddy earth, but there were no holes in or under the fence. Trusty must have climbed the woodpile again and jumped over the fence into our neighbor's yard.

I held the lantern out as far as I could. Sure enough, a half-dozen logs had fallen from the top of the pile into the yard.

If Trusty had left the yard, he'd have headed for Water Street. I worked there, and Mr. Chase's butcher shop on Union Wharf was his favorite stop. Mr. Chase always gave him a treat. But no one would be at the butcher shop at this time of night.

"Ma?" I called up the stairs leading to our sleeping chambers. "Trusty's gotten out. He's probably headed toward the river. I'm going after him."

Ma came to the top of the stairs. "Do be careful, Joe. The fog and black ice will be worse on the piers than here."

"Trusty could slip into the Sheepscot."

"As could you. Step sharply."

"I will, Ma."

By now, even the mud on the empty streets was freezing. Most people in Wiscasset were safe and warm behind shuttered windows glimmering with oil lamps. The telegraph office and taverns were open, but they weren't close to where I guessed Trusty'd gone.

I held the lantern ahead of me, low, hoping the light would be reflected in invisible patches of ice on the narrow street. I skidded twice, and once slid and landed on my rear, spilling some of the oil from the lamp onto the frozen mud. The oath that came from my lips was not the sort I'd print in a family newspaper.

Long wharves met the land at Water Street. Shops and stalls there sold everything needed by the mariners and their vessels that sailed from the Sheepscot River. A few tradesmen lived above the stores, but at this time of night the southern end of the street was left to the tides and bats and night birds.

Now was the season when small vessels were pulled out of dry dock for summer, shipyards launched winter-built vessels, and ships set sail for foreign seas after wintering in port for repairs and time ashore for their captains and crews.

"Trusty!" I called out, peering ahead through the mists. "Trusty, come!"

The fog was heaviest here, in some places obscuring vessels and piers entirely. Swirling in lacy patterns, it teased me, lifting momentarily to reveal a docked ship or shuttered shop. I aimed my lantern so its light wouldn't be reflected in the mist. I'd been confused by shimmering ghostlike reflections in past fogs. I shivered, remembering.

Every few minutes I called again. "Trusty!"

If there were spirits in Wiscasset, they would be here now. If the dead came back to what they loved, then Ethan would be here, for sure. He'd loved the sea, and the soft mysteries of the fog.

"Trusty! Come!" The masts on the ships anchored in the harbor looked like a forest of leafless trees that appeared and then disappeared. Where was that dog?

Arf!

The sound wasn't close by. Maybe I'd only heard the low moan of a ship's rigging grinding against its mast.

"Trusty!"

ARF!!

This time I was sure: The bark was louder. I ran, carefully, toward the sound—toward the corner where Water Street met Main Street, and then Main Street became the red Long Bridge across the Sheepscot. In winter ice gathered around the bridge's pilings, and the wooden bridge itself became a treacherous pathway of thick ice. Even now, black ice from the dampness and fog would cover the boards, making them slick and dangerous. Trusty wouldn't have ventured onto the bridge, would he? A small dog could easily slip off into the icy salt water.

I called again. "Trusty?"

The answering bark was soft, but close by. I turned. For a moment the fog cleared, and it looked like the mist circled around a slight figure standing in the doorway of Mr. Pinkham's stationery store.

Then Trusty ran toward me, feet slipping wildly on the ice but tail wagging like mad. I dropped the lantern and swept him up in my arms, burying my face in fur wet with fog. His tongue lapping my face was rough and warm.

"There you are! You should have known better than to run away in the fog!" Trusty's whole body shook with delight.

48

"I can see he's your dog." The white-hooded figure stepped carefully out of the mist.

"What are you doing out in this weather?" I asked, staring. "It's dangerous on the streets."

Nell Gramercy laughed. "You're here, too! I couldn't stand being inside any longer. I wanted to see the river in the fog."

"There isn't just fog. There's black ice—ice you can't see. You'd best get back to your inn."

Nell hesitated. "Your dog . . . you called him Trusty? Trusty found me. I was staring at the river. It changes, you know, every second. I saw faces there, in the mist."

I gulped. "I've lived here all my life. I assure you, there are no people on the river now, miss."

Nell shrugged. She was as small as I remembered; her head only came up to my shoulder. "Sometimes there are people no one else sees. What is across the bridge?" She took another step toward me and slipped on the ice. I grabbed her arm to keep her from falling.

"I'm afraid I came north unprepared." She stuck out her foot, displaying a stylish leather boot clearly not meant to be worn on icy streets. "I expected April to be warmer." Even in the gray mist I could see her blush. "Before you got here I tried to walk back up the hill, but I slipped. And fell."

She held out her left hand, as a child would do to show a sore spot. The palm of her thin white kid glove was torn. Kid gloves sold in our store were expensive. Most women in town wealthy enough to own a pair saved them for elegant occasions.

"I'll get you back to the inn," I said. "That's Long Bridge—longest bridge in the State of Maine, folks say—more than three thousand feet long. It goes over to Davis Island, in Edgecomb. You can't see the island now, because of the fog."

"Do many people live there? I thought of walking across before I found out how icy it was."

"A few families. And Fort Edgecomb is there. It was built to protect Wiscasset during the War of 1812."

"It's old, then."

"People talk about fixin' it up, but never seem to do so. It's a nice spot for a picnic. Or a game of hide-'n'-seek for children in summer."

Nell shivered. "I'm cold. I'll let you help me to the inn. I'm staying at the Mansion House."

I put Trusty down, hoping he'd stay with us. Nell took my arm as though she were a grown woman, not a twelve-year-old. No one had ever taken my arm before. I sure hoped I didn't fall on my rear again while she was trusting me to help her stay upright.

I held the lantern and we started carefully up the hill.

"I should introduce myself," she said. "I'm Nell Gramercy, from Albany, New York. No one knows I left the inn. My aunt and uncle think I'm resting. They'd be furious with me if they knew I'd left. I'm embarrassed at having to ask for help, but I don't know how to get back up the hill without falling again."

"I'm Joe Wood, from Wiscasset, Maine." I grinned, thinking how Charlie would howl if he could see me now. "I own a newspaper and print business in town. I know who you are. I've heard you can talk to the dead."

50

"Spirits of the departed come to me," Nell corrected. "I don't know why, or how. It's been happening since I was very young."

"My father was at your spirit circle the other night. You delivered a message from my older brother, Ethan."

"I remember your father, and the spirit of your brother. Your brother was young when he moved on, wasn't he?"

"He was fifteen when he died."

"I'm sorry." She paused. "I had brothers, too, once. I hope the message helped your father."

I nodded. "It did. Pa seems to be sorrowing less. He's helping Ma at our store again."

"I'm glad. Spirits come to me because they're not at peace, or because they feel someone they left behind is not."

We made our way carefully up the street, Trusty following close behind.

"Then you really hear the voices of dead people?" I couldn't help but ask her directly.

"Not all the time. And I don't hear them exactly; I sense them," said Nell. "It's hard to explain. And it's very tiring. That's why I was lying down this afternoon. I had one of my headaches."

"Ma gets headaches. She drinks peppermint tea or powdered charcoal in water."

"Does that help her?"

"I guess. She doesn't have to lie down a lot."

"She's lucky. Sometimes my headaches last for days, and I can't eat or sleep. My uncle gives me medicine, but it doesn't take the pain away; it lifts me above the pain. Sometimes I wish I didn't have commitments to people. Then I could hide in a dark place for hours. This afternoon I felt a little better and hoped some fresh salt air would clear away the pain and shadows."

"Has it?"

"I guess it has." Nell smiled. "I've been so worried about getting back to the inn over the ice I haven't had a chance to think about my head. I must be better!"

Up the hill, a block ahead of us, several men were standing outside the telegraph office.

"Wait," Nell said, stopping. "Why are all those men there?"

"Waiting to hear the latest news from Charleston," I explained. "The telegraph office is in Mr. Johnston's store."

"Then take me to the back door of the inn, please."

"But that's half a block farther than the front door."

"I don't want anyone in town to see me. They might start asking me questions about the future, or about their loved ones. And my uncle will be sitting with his brandy and cigar in the tavern or lobby of the Mansion House. He'd be furious if he knew I'd gone out alone. The back door is best."

"How did you leave without his seeing you?"

Nell grinned and tightened her grip on my arm as we made our way across a patch of thick ice. "Down the back stairway and through the kitchen. My aunt was napping, and the maid told me how." She squeezed my arm. "They don't usually leave me alone. I've tried to get away on my own other times, but never managed before."

"Get away? You mean you can never leave your aunt and uncle?" Of course, girls had to stay closer to home than boys. But Nell was famous.

She traveled. Somehow I'd expected her to have more freedom than others.

"My aunt and uncle schedule my work so I have little spare time. They say they're protecting me from this world, so I can more innocently speak with the next." She grimaced. "Perhaps so. But I miss the freedom I had growing up, when my spirits were free to come and go as they pleased, not as my uncle demanded. And I was free to explore this world as well as the next." She had wide blue eyes. "I love the scent of the sea, and the softness of the fog, here. But if I don't return to the Mansion House soon, I fear my uncle will be very angry." She quickly corrected herself. "He'll be concerned about my well-being."

"Then, Miss Gramercy, I shall conduct you back to the kitchen."

"It's Nell," she said. "I get so tired of people calling me 'Miss Gramercy.' I'd like to be just plain Nell to someone besides my aunt and uncle! And, after all, you've saved me from being frozen by the river."

Trusty barked.

"And, of course, Trusty, you must call me Nell, too."

What would Charlie think? Miss Gramercy—Nell—seemed just like anyone else. Excepting she talked to dead folks, of course. But the way she spoke about it, she could have been describing the color of her hair, or how tall she was. It was just part of her, something she could do.

How could I write an article saying Nell was tricking everyone if she really *did* hear voices? Some religious folks said God talked to them, and no one said they were crazy. How was this any different?

I slept little that night, trying to puzzle it out.

WISCASSET HERALD

POST OFFICE BUILDING, SECOND STORY,
WATER STREET, WISCASSET, ME.

WAR! WAR! WAR!

THE CONFLICT COMMENCED!

WHOLE COUNTRY IN SHOCK

AT 4:27 on the morning of April 12 of this year, 1861, the Confederate battery at Fort Moultrie in Charleston, South Carolina, now considering itself a part of the Confederate States of America, commenced firing on Fort Sumter, a United States military facility located on an island in Charleston Harbor.

United States Major Robert Anderson and the seventy United States soldiers stationed at Fort Sumter returned fire.

Provisions to support our men at Fort Sumter are in transit from the fort at Norfolk, Virginia, but are not expected to arrive for several days.

As we go to press, heavy shelling continues on both sides. It is not known if there are any casualties.

The Nation prays for the brave patriots at Fort Sumter.

Chapter 11

Saturday, April 13, 5:30 p.m.

"I can't believe you actually talked with her last night!" Charlie said, as he carried another chair from the dining room to the ballroom of the Mansion House. He and I had press passes for Nell Gramercy's meeting, but Charlie's father hadn't been impressed with our importance. He'd recruited us to set up the room for the event. "You talked with her alone. Without me!"

"I couldn't exactly ask her to stand outside in the cold while I ran to get you." I lined up the chairs in the eighth row. "Besides, we weren't alone. Trusty was with us."

Charlie parted the drapes and looked out at Main Street. "The crowd that was outside the telegraph office has starting moving this way. Looks like no change in the news from South Carolina."

"Good. Our front page says the fighting continues. I've been worried it would end and we'd have to print a special edition, or change the whole front page."

Charlie leaned to the right so he could see up Main Street. "I see Owen, over by the town pump. Your idea that he should sell copies in the street before the meeting was brilliant. Four or five people are in line to buy *Herald*s right now."

I clapped Charlie on the shoulder. "More money toward what I owe Mr. Shuttersworth! You were right about those interviews, asking people what they thought about the situation down south. People *do* like to see their names in the newspaper."

"Good thing we printed extra copies. It's not every day we have a battle in Charleston *and* a spiritualist in town, that's for sure." Charlie looked around. "Father said we should put seventy chairs in here. I think we're done."

"Did you look closely at the room before we started moving the chairs in? You know—to see if Nell or her uncle had changed it in any way?" Nell hadn't acted as though she was a fraud when we'd talked, but there was no harm in investigating.

"Nothing's suspicious. The drapes were drawn, and the oil lamps lit. The stove's full of wood. This room is always set up this way for an evening gathering."

"What about Nell's chair and table?"

"They're the same ones used in the dining room." Charlie looked around the room again. "I'll tell Father we've finished so he can be sure everything is exactly the way Mr. Allen requested."

I'd only been on the second floor of the Mansion House a few times. The ballroom was directly across from the dining hall. To the left were doors leading to other, smaller rooms. I peeked into an empty sitting room elegantly wallpapered in bright red-and-blue stripes. Next to it was another parlor, this one painted in green with a pattern of leaves stenciled on the walls. A love seat and several chairs were arranged with two card tables, one of them set for a game of chess. At the very end of the hallway the door of a third room was partially closed. I was about to look in when I heard voices. I stopped, just in time.

I could hear Nell's voice clearly.

"My headache's better, thank you, Uncle Horace. But I'm still light-headed."

"Horace, you must keep this grand assembly of yours short tonight, or Nell will be worse tomorrow. I cannot believe you engaged private sessions for her on a Sunday. You know without rest her headaches will get worse again."

"My dear, I'm only doing what's necessary. We're stuck in this dreary town until we have enough funds to take us to Nell's engagement in New York City. That journey will not be inexpensive. Talk of war is filling coaches and inns."

I moved closer to the door so I wouldn't miss a thing.

"Why can't we remain here a while?" Nell was pleading. "I could do one session each day instead of four. That way I could rest as well as support us."

"We can charge three times as much for your services in a city like New York. Not to mention that in a small town like this one, you'll quickly run out of customers. Curiosity seekers will disappear. New clients are easier to find in a city."

I wanted to peek into the room, but was afraid I'd be seen.

Her aunt spoke again. "Still, Horace, you must keep tonight's session short. For the girl's sake."

"Hush, woman; it won't be long. I'll tell everyone the truth: Communicating with spirits is wearing for someone so weak and young. If she looks pale and confused, so much the better for the act. If we're lucky, the people whose questions she doesn't get to will pay more to come back next week, to get their answers in individual sessions."

"Perhaps then, Uncle, you will not schedule any sessions on Monday? Please . . . So I can rest?" Nell said. "You know how exhausted I am after I've been with the voices, and with four sessions tomorrow—"

"You're stronger than you think," her uncle replied. "You always say you won't be able to continue, but I've seen you perform when you could hardly stand up. You can do it. As it is, I've scheduled only one Monday meeting so far, and it's not a spirit circle. You're to be interviewed by two local boys who call themselves newspapermen. They publish a little weekly paper, and they plan to write an article about you, my dear. All you have to do is be your most charming. If you're not feeling your best, that's fine. Another article on your delicacy and sensitivity and being attuned to the spirit world can only bring in more customers."

"What are the boys' names?" Nell said.

Was she wondering if I was one of them? I'd told her about the *Wiscasset Herald*.

"I can't recall. But they'll be here tonight, so smile your sweetest at any young men in the audience. They printed up the broadsides for us, so I gave them press passes."

"I'd like to lie on the couch a little longer to clear my mind before I begin," said Nell.

"You do that. Sarah, give Nell some of her medicine. It will help the spirits come to you, my dear, and dull your pain. In the meantime, I'll go down to the lobby to greet your public."

I raced back to the ballroom to make sure Mr. Allen didn't catch me listening outside the door.

Charlie was there already.

"Where have you been? Father said the room's fine, and that we could have cider and molasses cookies in the kitchen while we're waiting for the meeting to start. But I told him we wanted to be here early to see who comes and what they say. We might be able to quote someone in our article."

"Charlie," I said, "we need to talk. Now."

Chapter 12

Saturday, April 13, 6:30 p.m.

"What is it, Joe?"

"I overhead Nell talking with her aunt and uncle. She's not well. And her uncle's forcing her to have these sessions to make money, even though they make her headaches worse."

"Did you hear anything about how she does it? How she tricks people?"

"No, nothing like that! They just talked about how sick she felt, and how Mr. Allen had scheduled her to keep doing sessions." I lowered my voice even further. "And, he told her about us."

"Us?"

"He told Nell she had to talk with two young boys—not young men, Charlie, but *boys*—on Monday. That they had a little local newspaper. That she should charm them so they'd write a nice article and she'd have more customers." I smacked my fist into my other hand. Hard. "I publish a real newspaper. He made it sound as if we were children playin' with a toy printing press."

"Then I suppose we'll have to show him we're more than that, won't we? By writing an article that won't bring her paying customers. By exposing her and her uncle and aunt as frauds."

My mind whirred with confusing ideas. "Her uncle may be cruel, but that doesn't mean she's a fraud. We have no proof."

"Not yet—but we will have. I'm sure of it."

People were beginning to gather in the hall outside the ballroom.

"We'll listen and take notes, and watch what happens," said Charlie, taking out his pad. He grinned. "Monday we'll meet with your friend Nell, but she won't be able to charm us, no matter how hard she tries. You'll see!"

He went and sat down. We'd agreed we wouldn't sit together, so we could see the room from different angles.

All I could think was that if we wrote a story saying Nell was a fraud, then how could she support herself?

What would happen to her then? How would she feel if we wrote that she *didn't* hear the spirits she'd told me were a part of her life?

And how would she support herself if no one believed her?

Perhaps most important, what would her uncle do?

Chapter 13

Charlie sat on the side of the ballroom, near the back. I sat in the third row.

I knew most of the people who'd gathered, although a few, like the heavy, bearded man sitting in the first row, were strangers. The towns-people looked at each other self-consciously as they came in and found seats. Death was a mystery, and they were here to find out whether Nell was able to communicate with those behind its curtain.

I pulled out my paper and pen in case I wanted to take notes.

Charlie might be right about Nell's being a fraud, or he might be wrong, but I was sure Nell's uncle was controlling her. Maybe even making her ill. I'd printed an antislavery lecture for Reverend Merrill in January which said no man should have power over another. Nell wasn't being allowed to make decisions about her own life.

But could a twelve-year-old girl know what was right for her? Wasn't that the responsibility of the adults in her family—especially the adult men? On the other hand, would a responsible uncle make Nell support him?

I was trying to figger it out when Nell's uncle entered the room and placed a basket on the front table. He introduced himself to those of us who were already seated, shaking the hands of the men and nodding politely at the ladies. As he spoke with each person in the audience, he handed them a sheet of paper.

When the room was full Mr. Allen raised his hands for attention. "Good evening! Miss Gramercy and my wife and I have been enjoying our stay in your fine village, and have been honored to meet so many of you during the past week."

People in the audience nodded and smiled or looked at each other as if to say *Yes, that's us he's talking about. We've met Nell and Mr. Allen.* How many spirit sessions had Nell held in the past week? She might well have seen most of these people in separate or small group sessions already. That would mean she already knew their interests and concerns and what their questions might be. Or had Mr. Allen met these people at the tavern—or at least heard some local gossip there?

"This evening's session is one for questions and answers. Miss Gramercy will be unable to spend a great deal of time on any one question, but she's prepared to continue as long as her strength holds up. These sessions, as many of you already know, are very exhausting for Nell. She's only twelve years old, and of the weaker sex. Communicating with those in another world drains her energy."

Mr. Allen picked up the basket from Nell's table. "If you have questions you would like her to answer, she asks that you write them down, fold your sheet of paper twice, and place it in this basket as I walk among you. When I've gathered all your questions, she will join us."

Everyone set to writing. I hesitated, and then wrote, *Nell, why does your uncle control your life?* on my sheet and placed it in the basket as Mr. Allen passed. As the last questions were collected, Nell entered the room, dressed, as always, in white.

She was pale. How much did her head ache? I hoped the medicine her aunt had given her had helped.

"Good evening." She smiled and sat in her chair at the front of the room. "I'm pleased to see among you many I've had the pleasure of speaking with more intimately in the past week." Her eyes went from one person in the audience to another. It seemed like she smiled particularly at me, but she might have been smiling at everyone. Or just being "charming," as her uncle had directed her to be.

"My uncle is holding the questions you've written, but I know that many of you have questions you have not placed in the basket. Many of you have wondered how I communicate with the spirit world, and whether or not I am doing so legitimately. So, before I begin, let me tell you a little about myself."

People around me leaned forward in their seats. They didn't want to miss a word of what Nell had to say.

"Since I was a young child, I've been blessed with the gift of sensing the presence of those in another world. I cannot always hear their words distinctly, or see the physical bodies of those who speak to me. But something in me resonates, like a fine wire being tuned, and what is in their mind enters mine. I do not always know the meaning of what I sense. It is often up to those for whom the messages are intended to interpret their meaning." She paused.

"Tonight, instead of simply reading the questions you have asked and answering them, I will try to enter your consciousness, and those of the spirits you wish to contact, and match your questions with answers. Please be patient with me. Often I cannot work quickly. I will open and read your questions aloud only after the spirits have given me their answers."

What she was promising to do sounded impossible. I saw other people in the audience shake their heads, or whisper to each other in doubt. How could Nell or her spirits answer questions without knowing what the questions were?

Nell raised her hands. "Please help me concentrate by keeping silent." She closed her eyes for a moment and then opened them, staring into the distance.

"She isn't blinking!" whispered Mrs. Evans, who was sitting in front of me.

"Shhh!" said her husband.

What was Nell seeing? She became paler, and her eyes held the startled look I'd once seen on an owl sitting on a pine branch. When she spoke her words didn't vary in tone. She sounded as though she was repeating something she'd heard.

"Amy sends her love, and hopes her son and the young woman he has chosen will be married soon."

The bearded man in the front row jumped up, startling everyone. "That's my ma—Amy! And I'm about to ask Jenny, my girl, to be my wife! See? Here!" The man pulled a small red velvet sack from his jacket pocket and emptied it into his other hand, displaying the shiny ring inside to the audience. "I'm headin' for Belfast and the woman of my dreams tomorrow. Thank you, Ma! Miss Gramercy, thank you!"

The man walked quickly to the door, waving the ring as he went. "She can do it! She tells the truth!"

Others in the audience shifted in their seats. Who was that man? Whoever he was, he was certainly pleased with Nell's message.

Nell pulled a paper out of the basket and read it out loud: "Shall I propose marriage to Miss Jenny Holden?"

She had certainly answered the bearded man's question.

Nell waited for silence and then went back into her trance-like state again. Her next words were, "Robert and Lizzie are safe and happy, and wish their mother to know that."

Mrs. Smith, in the third row, burst into tears. "My babies! My dear babies!"

Nell chose another folded paper. "Are my children well in Heaven?"

Throughout the room people leaned forward, amazed at what Nell was doing, and the responses she was getting.

Her voice was strained this time. "Your time for childbearing is not over. Your son will have another brother."

Mrs. Bascomb, Owen's mother, gasped and grabbed her husband's hand.

Nell read from another folded paper: "Is my son fated to be an only child?"

Thank goodness Owen had not come! Nell had brought a very personal message to his parents. Mr. and Mrs. Bascomb were not a young couple. Would Owen really have another brother? Only time could prove Nell wrong or right, but tonight, his parents were clearly thrilled.

Then Nell paused and seemed to look right at me. "No one living person controls a life. Only the spirits know what shall be."

That had to be Nell's answer to my question.

She raised a folded sheet of paper. "Why does your uncle control your life?"

It *was* my question! How had she known?

Mr. Allen stood up and glared at the audience. "That question was inappropriate. Miss Gramercy has been suffering from exhaustion and headaches. Since this audience clearly does not respect her abilities, she will now retire to her room."

Nell opened her mouth, as if to say something, but her uncle pulled her up and pushed her toward the door closest to the table. The astonished crowd was still sitting down when the side door to the ballroom swung open.

"*News!*" It was Miss Averill, the telegraph operator. Her voice was high and loud. "News of our brave troops, just in over the wires: Fort Sumter has fallen! Fallen to the Confederates!"

Chapter 14

The room fell silent.

"Fort Sumter fell at 2:34 this afternoon, after thirty-four hours of fighting," Miss Averill announced, loudly enough so all could hear.

"How many killed?" someone called from the back of the room.

She shook her head. "No one on either side."

Nell was still standing a few feet away from the door, and was about to speak when her uncle pushed her toward the door. He turned back to the stunned crowd.

"If your questions were not answered tonight, you can blame the impertinent idiot who had the audacity to question my loyalty to my niece. She will only be available for private consultations during the next week."

But by that time no one was paying attention to him.

Fort Sumter had fallen. The Confederates had won. The ballroom filled with noisy conversations as people stood and put on their wraps. The headline wrote itself inside my head: FORT SUMTER LOST.

"How awful—how insulting to Miss Gramercy, that someone asked her that question," I heard one man say. His voice seemed very far away.

"That was the shortest evening's entertainment I've ever paid for. And for twenty-five cents," complained another.

"She would have stopped anyway after Miss Averill came in. Fort Sumter's fallen. We're at war now."

"What's Lincoln going to do?"

"Guess Captain Tucker, and anyone else with business in the South, just lost their incomes," said another man. "Buy you an ale at the tavern?"

"You will not," interrupted a woman's voice. "I'm taking my husband home. If President Lincoln starts calling up troops, who knows what will happen. I want my Henry to be home as long as possible."

"What wonderful things Miss Gramercy knew," said another woman nearby. "I must register for one of her private sessions. Who knows what messages she might have for me?"

War. That was all I could focus on. I moved through the crowd toward the door, passing two women congratulating Mr. and Mrs. Bascomb on the impending birth of their child. Normally such an event would not be spoken of until the possibility of a child being born was clearly visible, but Mrs. Bascomb was blushing and nodding. Nell must have been right, although it would be months before anyone would know if her prediction of another brother for Owen was correct.

Charlie came up behind me. "What a night! Nell Gramercy answering questions like that, and Fort Sumter falling! I only wish she'd been able to answer more questions, so we'd have had more time to figure out what she was doing. Who do you think asked such a brazen last question?"

Not waiting for an answer, Charlie led the way to his small room, where he began pacing from one side to the other. "When will they start signing men up to fight?" he wondered out loud. "What will happen to the soldiers captured in Charleston? What will President Lincoln do? Where will the next battle be?"

"Hold on, Charlie!" If Charlie got all churned up, he'd be of no use to me—and I needed his help. "We got this week's issue of the *Herald* out just in time. No one will fault us for not including the results of the battle. But now we have to write up another special edition, get it out tomorrow if we can."

"You can count on me," said Charlie, finally sitting down. "We'll want it out before we do the interview with Nell Gramercy on Monday. Which reminds me: I wonder who asked her that last question?"

"I did," I told him.

"What?"

"I asked her the question about her uncle that made him so angry."

"But why? Why did you ask her that in public?" asked Charlie. "We're going to talk to her Monday. Now her uncle knows someone thinks he's running her life."

"Well, he is," I said. "But, more important, you want to prove she's a fraud. How can we do that without evidence? She spoke for such a short time tonight. We didn't find out anything. Although she did say that she'd talked with some of the people in the room before; maybe she'd already met the people whose questions she answered. If so, she'd have known their concerns."

"Who was that first man whose question she answered—the one with the beard?" asked Charlie.

I shook my head. "I've never seen him before. He said he was headin' to Belfast. Few people are traveling by road this time of year."

"And he said he'd be going tomorrow. There's only one way he could do that and not be delayed by the mud." Charlie looked at me.

I nodded in agreement. "By water."

Without saying another word we left the Mansion House and headed down to the north end of Water Street. We passed groups of men talking about the defeat at Fort Sumter.

There was no sign of the bearded man from Belfast. "He's probably at one of the taverns," Charlie said. "If he's a fisherman or a mariner, he'll no doubt be at Bailey's. That's the one closest to the wharves."

We both hesitated. Neither of us wanted to admit it, but our parents would be furious if they heard we'd gone into the disreputable public house owned by Major Ben Bailey. Maine, of course, is a dry state. Whiskey can't be sold except for medicinal purposes, by doctors or pharmacists. Folks order it shipped from Massachusetts for personal imbibing.

Other taverns in town respected the law by having men bring their own liquor in and "renting" glasses, or by selling food and "giving" whiskey away with meals. Not Major Bailey. His customers were mostly visiting mariners and those that were down and out. He sold whiskey openly. Sheriff Chadbourne closed him down now and again, but Pa'd told me that most upright Wiscasset folks liked the way things were. Bailey's Tavern kept rough and rowdy mariners down on the north end of Water Street, away from the rest of town. The gentlemen and ladies who lived up on High Street liked it that way.

"We're newsmen," said Charlie defiantly. "We need to interview that man from Belfast."

I was younger than Charlie. I couldn't show him I was more than a little afraid of this place. When we reached Bailey's Tavern, I pushed open the door.

The inside of the low-ceilinged room was dark with tobacco smoke and stank of whiskey and rum and hard-living men. Some stopped their conversations to look at us curiously.

"Up past your bedtime?" jibed one mariner with a wide red scar on his left cheek.

"Does your mother know where you are?" asked another, raising his tankard in our direction.

"We're seeking a man headed to Belfast," I said, raising my voice above the din. "Has a full, dark beard, and was up to the Mansion House an hour or so ago."

"What're you wanting with him?" answered a deep voice from the corner.

I turned. It was the man we'd been looking for. We made our way through the crowd, who'd quieted down to hear what we had to say.

"Could we talk with you for a few moments?" asked Charlie. "It's about Nell Gramercy."

"Lovely young lady she is, indeed," said the man. "And her uncle, a real gentleman. Supplied us all with rum this night, he did."

Charlie and I looked at each other.

"What do you mean, supplied you all with rum?" I asked.

"Earlier this week I was down to the wharves, checking my vessel, like any mariner would in this weather, when that citified Allen fellow came up to me. He inquired whether I knew many folks in town. I told him, no, I hailed from Belfast, but was tied up here due to business concerns. So he asked if I'd like to be making some hard cash. I said I was willing. He said I wasn't to tell anyone. But the money's been exchanged and drunk by now, so what's he to do?"

"What did he pay you for?"

"He gave me this fancy ring," the sailor said, taking the velvet sack out of his pocket and showing the boys the ring within. Up close they could see it wasn't real—only gold-painted tin.

"He told me as how his niece wanted to impress folks in town, so he asked me to get all excited, like, about what she said, and pretend it was a message from my mum." He grinned. "Paid me ahead of time, and it worked real well, I'd say. Always had a taste for the stage, I have. And I was back here at Bailey's by quarter past the hour."

He stood up and staggered a few steps toward the boys. "That answer your questions, young fellows?"

"Yes," I said. "Thank you."

"If you'd like, you could buy me another drink, you know. To thank me real good. Allen's money disappeared faster than I planned."

"We don't have any money," said Charlie, backing toward the door but taking out his notebook. "What's your name? We write for the local newspaper, and we'd like to use you as a source."

"Name's Daniel Obadiah Jacobs," said the man, breathing heavy fumes in our direction. "And 'Esquire' would look real good in print, too."

"Thank you again," I said as we rushed out the door and back onto Water Street, the laughter of the men inside following us.

We'd run a few steps down Water Street and were on Main before Charlie spoke.

"That's our proof, Joe—proof that Nell's performance this evening was staged."

I had to agree.

"At least the first part of it was. You were right; her uncle planned it." I hated to think Nell had lied to me. "And maybe she'd met with those other people earlier, and could guess what they'd be asking, too. But how did she know what folded question she'd pick next? And how did she know what *I* asked?"

Chapter 15

Sunday, April 14, morning

"The newspaper can wait this once," Ma had said firmly. "With the world turning upside down, this is no time to be skipping church services. No discussion." So instead of heading to the *Herald* office as early as I'd planned on Sunday morning, I was stuck going to church with Ma and Pa.

To be straight with you, they only knew I needed to get the extra edition out for its news value. They didn't know I had only eight days left until Mr. Shuttersworth drove up in his wagon to collect his money—or my press. I didn't want their pity, or their money. The *Herald* was my business. I had to manage it myself.

Yesterday's *Herald* had sold forty-six extra copies, so that was ninety-two cents, and the business cards for Mr. Dana had brought in $2.60. My account book now read $46.40. But how would I get the remaining $18.60 in only eight days?

I hoped God wouldn't mind if I snuck in an extra prayer for a small personal miracle. I figgered it wouldn't hurt none, and I could use all the help I could get. April 22 was looming close.

Seemed like everyone in town was thinking like Ma and Pa. The Congregational Church was full to overflowing. Reverend Merrill had hung the largest flag he could find above the entrance, so we all walked beneath the Stars and Stripes as we filed inside.

Uncertain Glory

No one questioned whether church and state should be separate on this April morning. Most folks in Wiscasset were churchgoers, and we were all patriotic citizens. What conflict could there be?

Clearly Reverend Merrill saw none, as he prayed for our soldiers and for those misguided souls in the Confederacy. He prayed for President Lincoln and Vice President Hamlin, and for the Cabinet, and for all the senators and representatives, and for Governor Washburn up in Augusta. He prayed for peace, and for the healing of our nation without bloodshed. We all sang "Am I a Soldier of the Cross?" as we left services.

I was itching to get down to my office, but no one else outside the church seemed in any hurry to rush off. Most Sundays folks chatted on the Green after services before leaving to fix Sunday dinner. Today a group of boys had found sticks and were racing about, pretending to shoot Confederate soldiers. About a dozen men headed directly from the church down toward the telegraph office. Had more news come in? I hoped Charlie'd checked. He hadn't been in church. How long would Ma and Pa want me to stick close to them? We'd done our praying, and I was getting more edgy by the minute.

"Ma, can I go down to the *Herald* office now?" I finally asked.

"Go on home and change out of your good clothes first," admonished Ma. "And put something in your stomach when you're to home. I do wish you'd stay for a decent dinner one of these days. We've hardly seen you in the past week."

"The boy's getting out the news," said Pa, winking at me. "He's a man with a job. You get on, Joe. Your ma and I have some planning to do for the store. If this war lasts more than a few days, it's going to make a difference in what folks are going to be looking to buy."

"Bound to be shortages, too," Ma said. "The first stores to get orders in will make out best. We have to decide how much of our savings we'll gamble on what inventory," she added. "We'll see you when you finish up for the day."

"Thanks!" I said, taking off toward home before they changed their minds. I was at the *Herald*'s office within fifteen minutes.

Owen and Charlie had beat me there.

"News?" I managed to get out as I raced up the stairs and through the door, breathing deeply. "Any news?"

"Where've you been?" said Charlie sharply. "It's practically the middle of the afternoon. This is *your* newspaper, and I've had to set almost the whole first page myself. Did you think you could take Sunday off just because you felt like it?"

"My parents expected me to go to church with them. And it's not the middle of the afternoon. It's not even noon."

"Well, la-di-da. I didn't know you were so religious. I thought you were a newspaperman." Charlie slammed a type tray down. "Godfrey mighty! I've been here since early this morning. Even Owen has been here since eight o'clock. Nice of you to take the time to stop in—or maybe you thought you were helping by praying for us?"

"What needs to be done?" I knew better than to argue when Charlie was angry. I was just glad they'd both been there working.

"I've started printing a one-pager with today's news. Major Anderson surrendered, as expected. And there was one death at the fort. I had to rewrite the story twice as details changed, and then set the type by myself."

"I thought no one had died in the fighting," I said.

"No one did. But one of our gunners decided to give a last salute to the flag before the surrender. He was loading his gun when it exploded, and blew off his arm. He bled to death."

"How awful." I shook my head. "He died for no reason." I started re-filing pieces of type that Charlie had discarded and left on the table.

"What do you mean, 'no reason'? He died for his country," snapped Charlie. "What better death can there be?"

"A death that accomplishes something. That makes a difference to those still living," I said. "Not bleeding to death because your gun blows up."

"He died a hero," said Charlie, turning to me and standing a little too close for comfort.

Owen managed to squeeze between us. "Joe, while Charlie does the printing, would you help me hang the pages so they'll dry fast?" He was holding the rope we usually strung across the room.

"Of course I'll help, Owen." I stepped backward, avoiding a confrontation. "We all want to get that page finished as soon as we can. You've both done a great job this morning. I can't believe you worked so quickly."

"President Lincoln should make an announcement soon," said Charlie. "He'll tell us what he's going to do, and what he wants the country to do. After all, we're at war. Everything's going to be different from now on." Charlie started to print copies. "This is probably the most important time of our lives."

"That will mean a lot of special issues of the *Herald,* right?" said Owen. "We'll make a lot more money."

"We may," I said.

I hadn't yet told Owen about possibly losing the press; I'd hoped I would never have to.

"Special issues are just the beginning, Owen!" said Charlie. "There's no telling how different our lives are going to be from now on." He was grinning, working the press faster than I'd ever seen before. "Changes are coming, Owen. Just you wait and see! Nothing's going to be the way it was before Fort Sumter fell."

He made it sound as though war was the best thing that could have ever happened to us.

WISCASSET HERALD

POST OFFICE BUILDING, SECOND STORY,
WATER STREET, WISCASSET, ME.

FORT SUMTER LOST

DESPITE withstanding heavy bombardment from the Confederate battery for more than thirty-two hours, as a result of fierce fires burning throughout Fort Sumter, United States Major Robert Anderson and his troops in Charleston, South Carolina, were forced to surrender to forces led by Brigadier General P. G. T. Beauregard of the Confederate States of America in the early afternoon of April 13.

Major Anderson and his men evacuated what remained of the fort on Sunday, April 14, with full honors of war. Before leaving the island Major Anderson ordered the firing of a national salute to our nation's flag. Gunner Daniel Hough became the first man to lose his life on our side of the war when his weapon went off prematurely, blowing off his right arm and killing him instantaneously. Sparks from his gun's muzzle also ignited a pile of cartridges, causing several other men in the vicinity to be blown into the air and seriously injured.

After the salute, Confederate troops marched into the fort to occupy it, and raised the Confederate flag above the ramparts.

The Nation awaits further word from President Lincoln at Washington.

Chapter 16

Sunday, April 14, late afternoon

One of the first changes because of the war was that schools were to be closed on Monday. No one questioned the decision. This week families felt a need to stay close. Talk of the war was on everyone's lips as Owen and Charlie and I walked from home to home late Sunday afternoon, selling our one-page bulletin announcing the fall of Fort Sumter and Major Anderson's surrender.

Most people in town bought a copy.

"I'll be saving this," said old Mrs. Dunham. "I'll put it with my Bible. I suspect I'll be doing a lot of praying from now on—praying for all of us, and for our nation. For what'll be coming next." She reached out and hugged both Charlie and me, to our surprise and embarrassment.

"She didn't hug me," said Owen as we left her house.

"You're lucky. She smelled of salt pork and rancid whale oil," I told him as we headed for the next house.

"You're too young to be a soldier," said Charlie. "She hugged Joe and me because she thinks we might die in the war."

"Charlie! How can you think such things?" I said, glancing at Owen. He looked as though he was about to burst into tears.

"It's true," said Charlie. "We're not children. Owen's still a little boy."

Mrs. Dunham wasn't the last, either. Mrs. Chase and Mr. Young both advised Charlie and me not to join up until the situation was clearer. Mr. Giles, on the other hand, came to the door, rifle in hand, asking if we'd heard yet where a man could go to enlist.

"Haven't heard nothin' about that, sir," I told him.

"You will soon," Mr. Giles answered grimly. "And when you do, I'll be there. Those Southerners aren't going to mess with my country and get away with it. Not likely. And any man who's a patriot will be right there with me. You remember that, boys."

Trusty trotted along with us, occasionally barking at a passing horse or a darting squirrel. Everywhere there were exciting smells. He sniffed hay dropped from a rumbling farm wagon and ran after a barn cat, until I called him back.

"Maybe Dr. Cushman would like a broadside," said Owen. "He's a good doctor. Mr. Dana pulled out my Pa's tooth when it hurt real bad, and left part of the tooth behind. Dr. Cushman pulled out the rest of the tooth, and there was hardly any blood."

"We'll go to his office next," I agreed.

Dr. Cushman's office was in his home on High Street, near the church and the courthouse.

Most folks who lived in big houses on High Street were like Captain Tucker, and made their living from the sea. They'd built their homes where they could watch the ships in Wiscasset Harbor coming and going, their fortunes ebbing and flowing with the tides.

A few of the boys who'd been playing soldier that morning were still chasing each other from one side of the Green to the other.

"Don't you want to be playing with the others, Owen?" Charlie asked as we walked up the hill. "We can carry the rest of the bulletins. You don't need to stay with us when you could be having fun."

"I *am* having fun," Owen said. "I'm not little, like those boys. I can help you and Joe."

Trusty returned from investigating a trail that looked as though a rabbit had briefly emerged and then gone back to his lair.

"Owen, you're only nine. Some of those boys are older than you are. You can't just follow us around all the time," said Charlie.

Owen's smile vanished.

"You've been a big help today," I added quickly. "Charlie just wants to be sure we aren't keepin' you from your friends."

"They're not my friends," said Owen. "They're just boys." He looked away from the Green. "What did you and the spiritual lady talk about, Joe? When you met her on the street."

"We talked of the fog, and the black ice." Would I betray Nell if I told Owen and Charlie she'd fallen? "She wasn't dressed for Maine weather. We talked about that, and Trusty, and I walked with her back to the Mansion House. I wasn't with her long."

"Did you tell her your father'd been at one of her sessions?" Charlie asked.

"She remembered him. She said spirits came to her when they had important messages to give to people left behind. She said she'd been hearing spirits since she was very young—that talking with them was tiring, and she often had headaches."

"Could she talk with my brother, do you think?" asked Owen.

"I don't know. I don't think she can talk with everyone who's died. It has to be someone who needs to contact someone still living."

"I'd like to get a message from my brother," said Owen. "But he was so little. He didn't even talk much when he was alive. He probably doesn't have anything to say now."

"He's probably happy in Heaven," agreed Charlie. "And if he's happy, he doesn't need to reach anyone here."

Owen nodded.

Dr. Cushman's office was on the first floor of his grand, three-story house.

"Dr. Cushman, sir, would you like to buy a one-page bulletin with news about Fort Sumter?" I asked when he opened the door. Dr. Cushman's office was the only one like it in town. Stuffed robins and egrets and puffins and gulls and passenger pigeons and eagles, and even a large snowy owl that the doctor had shot, hung on the walls.

Owen shivered. "The birds all have eyes," he whispered to Charlie. "They're looking at me."

Dr. Cushman took a copy of the paper and handed me a penny. "Thank you. I'm impressed with how well you've been running that newspaper of yours."

"There's bound to be a lot of news now," Charlie put in, "with the war and all, and with Nell Gramercy in town, making predictions. We have an exclusive interview with her tomorrow."

Dr. Cushman frowned. "That young woman's presence in Wiscasset is an unfortunate folly. She's encouraging people to think they can contact the dead." He shook his head. "I have the sad job of ministering to people who are leaving us for the hereafter, and I have to say, I've never seen any of them return."

"They don't return. They just leave messages with Nell for people who loved them," I said. "She got a message from my brother Ethan, for my father."

The doctor looked at me. "I heard that, Joe. My wife was over to your family's store yesterday. She said your father was helping put merchandise out, and was feeling much better."

"He is," I replied, nodding.

"Sometimes recovery comes in strange ways," Dr. Cushman said. "But people need to understand that there's a line between the world of the living and the world of the dead." He looked out into the empty street. "Although you can't know the number of times I've wished I could make that line disappear, or at least change the moment it comes to one of my patients."

"I hope I never have to go to that doctor," said Owen, as we headed back down the hill. "When he fixed my father's tooth he came to our house. We don't have dead birds." He looked up at me. "Dr. Cushman won't shoot Gilthead, will he?"

"I'm sure he won't," I assured him. "Everyone in town knows Gilthead's a pet."

But I wondered whether Dr. Cushman would pay the Bascomb family a visit should Gilthead ever die of natural causes. I hadn't seen any parrots in Dr. Cushman's collection.

Chapter 17

Monday, April 15, morning

"Joe, Joe—come quick! There's trouble! Fighting down at the Custom House!"

I was rightening up the office after Sunday's work. I'd already made good use of the broom, and had just added the income from the Fort Sumter bulletin ($1.10, for a new total of $47.50) to the accounts book when Charlie's voice echoed up the stairs.

Fighting at the Custom House? Could Southerners have already attacked this far north? What weapons would they have? As I ran down the stairs to follow Charlie down Water Street, I felt in my back pocket for the knife Pa had given me last Christmas. It was meant for whittling, but most days I carried it with me, finding it handy for cleaning type and other chores. But what good would a small blade do in a war?

The street was full of men, women, and children running toward the massive stone and brick building down near Whaleship Wharf. A few men even waved muskets. Not many in town ever had need of weapons. Not before now.

A crowd had gathered in front of the Custom House steps. Mr. Cunningham, Wiscasset's customs collector, in charge of inspecting ships arriving from foreign ports, was holding the American flag high. That was the moment I realized it wasn't flying above the Custom House as usual.

"I refuse! I will not fly this sacred flag over a building representing a country that has declared war on its own states!" Mr. Cunningham shouted. "I care not what that so-called president of ours says! The Southern states should be reasoned with, not declared our enemy. Lincoln is wrong, and I will not follow a command against my principles!"

"Traitor!" screamed old Mrs. Fairfax from the crowd, shaking her cane at Mr. Cunningham. "Those Southerners fired on our boys! On United States soldiers!"

"She's right!" yelled Mr. Dana, the pharmacist. "Lincoln's our president. Raise the Stars and Stripes!"

"Traitor! Traitor!" The crowd took up the cry.

Without thinking, I found myself chanting along.

"I'd rather burn down this building than raise our sacred flag when it no longer represents the United States our forefathers created—the United States we love and honor!" shouted Mr. Cunningham.

"Try to burn down the building, you idiot!" yelled someone else. "The building's strong, like the Union, made of stone and brick. It won't burn because of one man's opinion."

"We're going to war just because some slave-lovers want to change the way other people live!" bellowed Cunningham, trying to be heard above the crowd. "Let people live the way they want to live! Every state should make its own rules! Why should we send our sons to fight in a place we've never even seen?"

I saw Owen's father moving to the back of the crowd.

"Because we're all Americans!" came from the crowd.

The chant of *Traitor! Traitor! Traitor!* began again, and the crowd began to surge up the steps, toward Mr. Cunningham, who backed up against the high Custom House doors, clutching the American flag to his chest.

A shot rang out.

Chapter 18

The crowd went silent at the sound of the gun.

"Godfrey mighty," Charlie whispered. His face was pale.

You wouldn't believe how quiet it was. No one seemed to know what had happened—or what might happen next. I felt hot, and then cold, and although I'm not usually a praying person, I found myself saying a silent prayer that war wouldn't come to Wiscasset.

Then Sheriff Chadbourne strode to the top of the Custom House steps, holding an old musket in his hand. It was smoking.

"Thom, either you raise that flag and do your duty as customs collector, or I'm bound to arrest you on grounds of civil disobedience."

Mr. Cunningham raised his chin high. "I won't collect customs for a country that makes war with itself over a states' rights issue."

Sheriff Chadbourne sighed. "Then you'll have to come with me." He looked down into the crowd. "Henry, come take our nation's flag from Thom here." Then he spoke to everyone. "Folks, show's over. The Custom House is closed for today. Anyone's got customs issues, see me at the courthouse." He took Mr. Cunningham by the arm and marched him through the crowd as some jeered.

"I'll bet he's taking him to the old jail on Federal Street," Charlie said.

"Likely," I nodded. The old granite building had been there since the War of 1812. It wasn't a place anyone wanted to spend a single night, let alone a longer stay. Still, it was the Lincoln County Jail, and jail wasn't supposed to be a place you looked forward to visiting.

Gradually the crowd broke up, as there didn't seem to be any more excitement at hand. Charlie and I started back toward the *Herald*'s office.

"Guess I've got the first story for my next issue," I said. "I didn't think I'd have a new story so fast."

"Have you thought of any questions for Nell?" Charlie asked. "Our interview's at one o'clock."

"I have a few," I told him. "Not many."

I wasn't looking forward to seeing Nell again, after what had happened Saturday night. It hadn't been the right place to ask my question, and with what the Belfast mariner had told us, I was more confused than ever about Nell and her voices.

"Let's get a list of questions together," said Charlie. "We should stop in at the telegraph office first, though."

Others had had the same idea. A crowd had gathered by the time we got there. Mr. Johnston was standing outside his store, delivering the news.

"President Lincoln has called upon the various states of the Union to contribute a total of seventy-five thousand volunteer members from the various state militias to suppress the Southern insurrection, such volunteer state militia to be dispersed within ninety days."

"Only ninety days, Joe! He thinks it's all going to be over in ninety days," said Charlie. "That's barely time for troops to rally and be trained."

"Who among us is going to be patriotic and save the Union?" someone in the crowd yelled.

No one answered.

"What's going to happen next?" I said quietly, more to myself than to Charlie. I knew one thing for sure: I had another bulletin to get out. If I didn't sleep, and if Charlie and Owen kept helping me, maybe I'd still be able to make Mr. Shuttersworth's deadline.

"I'm not sure," said Charlie. "I suspect there'll be a lot of talking and drinking in statehouses. Does Maine even have a militia? I'll bet Governor Washburn is figuring that out right now." He grinned and slapped me on the shoulder. "C'mon. We have to talk with your Miss Gramercy before the world changes again. She says she can see the future; maybe she knows what will happen next."

Chapter 19

Monday, April 15, 1:00 p.m.

"Miss Gramercy and Mrs. Allen are awaiting your arrival in the blue parlor," said old Mr. Turner. He owned the Mansion House, and had presided over the lobby there for as long as I could remember. I detected a twinkle of amusement in his dignified words, and I swear he winked at me as I passed him on my way up the wide front staircase.

No matter. The important thing was that Charlie and I were going to talk to Nell.

The blue parlor was the room in back of the ballroom—where the Allens and Nell had been Saturday night. We stood outside its door for a moment. Charlie spit on his hand and smoothed down his cowlick. I took a deep breath and tried not to be nervous.

Nell Gramercy was just a girl, wasn't she? She'd seemed normal enough when we'd talked on the street. I was more nervous at seeing her aunt than I was at seeing her. What if I said something wrong—or insulted her by asking the wrong question? What if her aunt said we had to leave, the way her uncle had called off her session Saturday night?

I told myself I wasn't nervous at all about talking to Nell Gramercy. Even if she was a girl who talked to dead people.

I screwed up my courage and knocked on the door.

"Come in," Mrs. Allen called.

Uncertain Glory

Nell was sitting on a love seat in front of the fireplace, dressed in her usual white, although today her shoulders were wrapped in a pale blue lace shawl.

Her aunt, a grand woman in every sense of the word, sat in the chair closest to the love seat. Her hooped skirt was made of brown watered silk. That silk was expensive. Ma only ordered it when one of the women up on High Street or their dressmakers requested it. Mrs. Allen indicated that Charlie and I were to sit on the two chairs opposite them.

"My uncle tells me you publish a newspaper here in Wiscasset," said Nell. Her eyes were very clear and blue. I hadn't noticed that before. She didn't look as though she had a headache today. While I hoped she'd say something about meeting me earlier, I knew she couldn't. Her aunt and uncle couldn't find out that she'd left the inn by herself.

"Yes," I answered. "I own a print shop, and publish the *Wiscasset Herald,* a weekly newspaper, as well as special editions when there's important news."

"You must be very busy now, with news of the war coming in at all hours," said Nell.

"Indeed," Charlie said. "We just heard that Lincoln has called for seventy-five thousand volunteers. And this morning there was a scuffle down at the Custom House. The local customs agent didn't want to raise the Stars and Stripes because he didn't support the president's position on states' rights."

"And yet you're taking the time to speak with me."

"Your story is of great interest to our readers," I said. "No one of your . . . sensitivities . . . has ever visited Wiscasset before. Can you tell us how long you've been in touch with spirits who've . . . passed over?"

"All my life, I think," said Nell. "Even as a very young child I remember hearing voices of people who were not physically in the room, and sometimes seeing visions that others did not. I learned not to mention these things, for fear others would think me mad."

"And what brought you to believe you were not?" asked Charlie.

"When I was six, my older brother Luke went skating on a nearby pond with some of his friends. I was helping Mother in the kitchen, and suddenly I had a vision that Luke and one of his friends were skating near ice that I somehow knew would not hold them. I screamed as I saw them break through the ice and flounder, and then, not come up. Of course, my mother was alarmed that I was so distraught. As soon as I'd calmed down, she listened, and sent one of my older sisters—for I was one of seven children—to bring Luke home, so I could see that all was well.

"My sister was gone longer than she should have been, so all at home were anxious. She brought Luke's body home on a board, along with the body of his friend. Both had drowned."

Charlie and I sat, horrified. And fascinated.

"After that, I was afraid when I saw things that hadn't happened yet, or were about to happen. And soon I began to hear from those who'd passed over. Many people were afraid of my gift. Others saw it as a blessing. My dear aunt and uncle, with whom I now travel, taught me to see it as a way of helping people on this side to understand their grief. To free themselves of guilt and sadness. To live full lives, until it's their turn to go to the other side."

As you can imagine, I was wondering what Nell's uncle had done to support himself and his wife before Nell had come to live with them. Did they even have a home? She hadn't mentioned one, other than the house she'd shared with her parents and brothers and sisters. She said one brother had died, but where were her other siblings? From all I'd seen and heard, it seemed that she and her aunt and uncle traveled all over the country, their lives revolving around Nell and her voices—and those who would pay for her services.

But Charlie and I weren't here to talk about her aunt and uncle.

"Can you see the future?" I asked.

"Sometimes I can; sometimes not. My gift is not one that can be depended upon. I've had gamblers beg for the results of horse races, or politicians, the results of elections. My gift does not answer those sorts of questions."

"What does it tell you about this war we're entering into?" asked Charlie, leaning forward.

"It says little," said Nell, looking at him sadly. "But I see a long tunnel, and much darkness."

"That proves your gift is not perfect," said Charlie, almost triumphantly. "President Lincoln has only called up the militia for ninety days. No one thinks it will take long to defeat the Confederates."

"Only time will prove anyone right," said Nell. "Whether they be spirits or presidents."

"And now," Mrs. Allen said, "I think we've tired Miss Gramercy enough. You boys should be able to write something up with what she's told you, and you have all that news about the war to write up, too.

Miss Gramercy has to rest. Communicating with spirits is exhausting, you know. Very exhausting."

As she spoke, Mrs. Allen rose and shooed Charlie and I out of the parlor before we could ask any more questions. I looked back as Mrs. Allen closed the door. Nell smiled and raised her hand to wave good-bye.

Charlie and I ran back down the main stairs, nearly crashing into a dignified couple walking up. We didn't stop until we were out on Main Street, causing several frowns from gentlemen and ladies in the lobby.

"We didn't ask anything about her family," Charlie said suddenly, as we slowed down.

"It said in the Boston newspaper that she was an orphan. Her parents must have died," I reminded him. "And when we were walking the other night, she said she'd *had* brothers—as though she didn't anymore."

"I guess she's lucky her aunt and uncle are taking care of her." Charlie shook his head. "You and I have both had people die in our families, but you still have your ma and pa, and I still have my father." He walked a few steps further. "And we didn't ask how she performs her tricks."

"She's very convincing, isn't she?" I asked, looking back at the Mansion House and wondering if Nell was looking down at us.

I was glad Charlie hadn't asked her about tricks. I remembered what she'd said at that first session—that you had to believe in them for spirits to come. I had a feeling her voices wouldn't have wanted their existence questioned.

"I guess she did give us enough to write up our interview," Charlie said begrudgingly, as we stood on the street.

That was when we noticed something happening up near the Village Green.

Chapter 20

Monday, April 15, mid-afternoon

Old Major Ben Bailey, whose tavern we'd visited Saturday night, and who'd fought in the Mexican War back in the 1840s, had set an old, red-painted pine table plumb at the very bottom of the Village Green. On either side of the table he'd planted poles firmly in the mud, and the Stars and Stripes waved from each one.

On the front of the table hung a large, crudely lettered sign:

ARE YOU A PATRIOT OR A COWARD?

SOLDIERS, SIGN UP HERE!

"C'mon!" said Charlie, heading up to the table, along with eight or nine other people who'd also been watching. What was Major Bailey doing? Was this an enlistment station? It didn't look likely.

"Stand back, men! I can only take one at a time!" Bailey said, grinning at the men crowding around his table. "I'm proud to see all my fellow Wiscasset citizens respondin' to our president's call to arms!"

"Hey, Ben," called Mr. Irons, over the hubbub. "What're you doing? We've received no directions for enlistments. I've heard Maine has no money to pay a militia, neither."

"True enough, Archie," answered the major. "But mark my words, we'll have all the answers we need any day now. And the sooner we start thinkin' about it all, and men start markin' their name on a piece of paper"—he waved a blank sheet in the air to demonstrate—"the sooner we'll have our marchin' orders."

"How many men do you think they'll be wanting from Wiscasset?" Charlie asked.

"As many as wants to go, I reckon," said old Mr. Ames from over to Union Street. "Wars gobble up young men, and too many don't come home." He shook his head. "Don't none of you be signing no papers, for Ben or nobody else, 'til you thinks it through and talks with yer families." He stomped off down the hill, muttering to himself.

"Don't be believin' what Mr. Ames said right off," said Major Bailey. "Mr. Lincoln's talkin' ninety days. That's barely enough time to get men enlisted and armed and move 'em south, much less get 'em to any battles. And battles is where war is fought, ain't it men?"

I looked from one excited man to another. Most were nodding in agreement, Charlie with them. War was battles, wasn't it? That's what history books said. Battle after battle after battle. And for every victory in battle, someone was defeated. History books said that, too. We'd already lost the first battle, at Fort Sumter.

"To be a part of them battles, you got to be one of the first on the list. It's true, what Archie said," Major Bailey said. "We got no directions as to how to do this thing, and we got no money to pay anyone. But who needs to be paid to be a patriot? We know our president says he needs seventy-five thousand men, and he needs 'em now. Our governor and representatives up to Augusta are prob'ly trying to figure it all out right this very minute. We can get a head start by havin' a list ready for 'em of all those men ready, willin', and able, right here in Wiscasset. Ready to go march just as soon as we know where to send 'em."

"The major's a character, for sure," a man in back of me said, "but he's making more sense than most I've heard today."

"Maybe," said a second voice. "But I'm not signing any piece of paper that takes me away from home without talking it over with my wife, that's for certain. If I did that, I'd have no home to come back to!"

"Good point!" said the first, and the two men walked away.

"So, who's goin' to be the first patriot to sign his name?" said Major Bailey. "Who'll it be?"

No one stepped up. The men looked self-consciously at each other.

"C'mon, men. I'd sign it myself if I didn't know bein' over seventy would disqualify me, no matter what requirements they come out with in Augusta!" Everyone laughed.

But suddenly the crowd fell silent as Edwin Smith, who lived up on High Street, stepped forward. "I'll sign your paper," he said. "I've already decided to enlist, no matter what directions are sent from Augusta. I'm twenty-three, and healthy. They'll want men like me. I'll be the first to sign your paper, Major Bailey." He bent down and signed with a flourish. "I'm certain Wiscasset will have no problem enlisting enough other brave men to defend our Union."

After he signed, Edwin Smith headed up the hill toward his home. "He's probably going to tell his mother," whispered Charlie.

"I sure hope so," I said. "She shouldn't hear it from anybody else."

Next to sign was George Pierce, a friend of Smith's. He was followed by an older man from the countryside I didn't know. Charlie asked his name, so we could put it in the paper as one of the first to declare his intentions to enlist. "Paul Cunningham," was the answer. "I hear my cousin Thom acted up some at the Custom House this morn-

ing. I'm bound to restore family honor by acting like a patriot this afternoon."

After Mr. Cunningham, Owen's father, John Bascomb, signed his
name, shaking hands with several other men in the crowd afterwards. I
grinned at Mr. Bascomb and shook his hand, hard.

But Mr. Evernon turned away and refused to shake Mr. Bascomb's
hand.

"It's people like you, Bascomb, that are the cause of this war," he
said. "If there weren't any Negroes in this country, we wouldn't be in
this situation, and none of us would be talking about leaving our families and risking our lives."

"If people in the South didn't treat people as property, then we
wouldn't be at war," said Mr. Bascomb. "I'm proud to live in a country
willing to fight to end slavery."

"*Humph*," said Mr. Evernon, and he spit on the ground near Mr.
Bascomb. "Slavery's no problem for us here in Maine; we did away
with it years ago. Why should we get involved with a states' rights issue
in the South? Why should we care what happens in South Carolina?"
He stepped toward Mr. Bascomb. It looked as though he was ready to
fight. "Why should Maine men lose jobs—why should they lose their
lives—because of something happening hundreds of miles away?" He
took another step toward Mr. Bascomb.

Mr. Bascomb didn't back up, but others stepped between them. As
Charlie and I watched, Mr. Evernon backed off and headed down the
street toward the tavern.

"You'll all see I'm right!" he called back over his shoulder. "Just
wait!"

A shadow had fallen on the afternoon. Some of the men talked quietly among themselves, and one or two talked with Mr. Bascomb, I noted. But not many. No one else signed Major Bailey's paper.

In a few minutes the crowd dispersed.

"Mr. Evernon works for Captain Tucker, doesn't he?" asked Charlie, as we headed down the hill to the *Herald*'s office on Water Street.

"He's the accountant for Tucker's business," I answered. "I expect there won't be much shipping to account for between here and Charleston and London as long as there's a war on."

"So he may not have a job much longer," Charlie pointed out. "Not that Mr. Bascomb has anything to do with that."

"We have to write up the interview with Nell," I reminded him, ready to change the subject. "And the call for militia troops."

"And what happened at the Custom House this morning," added Charlie. "It's going to be another long night."

Chapter 21

Monday night, April 15, late evening

Even with Owen's and Charlie's help, it took all of Monday afternoon and evening to write up the news, set it in type, and then print it on both sides of a two-page *Herald*.

"We'll meet back here at seven sharp tomorrow morning to distribute it," I decided. "We won't make any sales now, with most folks gettin' ready for bed."

Could I ask 2 cents for this bulletin instead of the 1 cent I'd been charging? Two cents was my usual charge for a full, four-page issue, but this bulletin contained historically important news. I'd taken notice when some people said they planned to keep our recent bulletins.

"Let's hope nothing else newsworthy happens tonight," said Charlie, pulling on his jacket.

Owen had been yawning for an hour.

Only a week ago Charlie'd complained that nothing ever happened in Wiscasset.

When I got home Ma and Pa were going over their final list of inventory items to order for the store. I peeked over Ma's shoulder.

"Will we need to order that much?" I asked. "President Lincoln said he's only calling up troops for three months' service."

The list included wool for blankets and coats, heavy thread for uniforms, boots, cheap soap, combs, brushes, handkerchiefs, shaving sets, small sewing kits, traveling writing boxes, eating implements, water-proof envelopes, and knives of all sorts.

"It's risky," Pa agreed. "But we're guessing Lincoln's being optimistic. He doesn't want the country to be scared about the prospect of a long war. These supplies are already hard to come by, and will be harder to get in the future. Every soldier needs to be equipped."

"Word is, the State of Maine has no money to do so," I said.

Ma nodded. "True enough. But that won't stop men from wanting to go, and families will do the best they can for their menfolk. We plan on having what we can here in the store to help them do that."

"Our order will go to Boston on the stage first thing tomorrow. We may not be able to get everything on our list, but we'll try," said Pa. "And Joe? I know you're busy with the paper, and all the news coming in—"

"That's where I was tonight," I interrupted. "I have another special edition coming out tomorrow morning. I brought you a copy." I handed one to Pa.

He glanced at the headlines. "You interviewed Miss Gramercy, I see. That's what I wanted to talk with you about. Your ma and I have an appointment to see her privately on Wednesday afternoon. Can you mind the store for us then?"

I'd done that many times in the past. "Of course. You're going to ask her to contact Ethan again?"

"We are," said Ma. "I can't help being curious. She's such a little thing, to have so very special a gift . . ." Ma pointed to the newspaper sheet. "Well, you've met her, so you know. I'm hoping she can put us in touch with Ethan one more time. She's brought so many wonderful messages to other people in town."

Pa reached over and squeezed Ma's hand.

"The world is so full of dreadful news these days. It would mean a lot to hear a good word from Ethan. A final good word." She looked at Pa, and then back at me. "You understand, don't you, Joe?"

I nodded. I hoped Nell and her voices could give them the answers they wanted to hear.

Ma went over to the stove. "I kept some biscuits and ham warm for your dinner. You look exhausted. Why don't you take this upstairs to eat as you're getting ready for bed?" She filled a pewter plate and handed it to me.

"Thanks, Ma," I said. "And don't worry; I'll take care of the store for you Wednesday."

Upstairs I pulled my crazy quilt around me and ate the warm dinner. I wished Ma and Pa had included me in their session with Nell. Would she be able to contact Ethan again? What would she say? I wanted to hear.

And what would Charlie say if he knew my family had scheduled a private session with Nell? What news would come about the war tomorrow?

Just a week ago life had seemed so simple.

Chapter 22

I slept restlessly, and was at the *Herald* office before anyone else on Tuesday morning.

"It'd be best if we split up." I pointed at the papers I'd divided into three stacks. "Charlie, you cover the businesses on Main Street and the houses north of Main. Owen, you take these down to the stores on Water Street and Fore Street. I'll take the homes south of Main Street, and the church and courthouse."

That would give Charlie the telegraph office, the taverns, and most of the busier sections of Wiscasset. He loved to gab, and knew most folks there. Owen could take homes and small businesses, and I'd go to the legal buildings, the wealthier section of town, and the churches. Between us, we'd cover the center of Wiscasset in an hour or two.

"Today we're charging two cents for the issue. It's a two-pager, with historic significance—one that our readers will want to keep. Do your best. We'll meet back here as soon as our papers are gone, or as soon as we've covered our territories."

Owen and Charlie nodded. "And keep your eyes open for any news."

The three of us grabbed our piles of *Herald* sheets and headed out. The early morning was cool, but bright sun promised it would warm up later. Streets that had been muddy days before were beginning to dry.

Uncertain Glory

Most people were curious about our interview with Nell, and wanted to know who had signed Major Bailey's "enrollment" sheet on the Green yesterday. Coins soon filled my pockets. Only one or two people complained about the 2-cent charge.

When we all got back to the office I'd add up the books again and see how close I was to the $65 I needed for Mr. Shuttlesworth. I walked faster. For the first time in days I was beginning to think I might reach my goal.

Almost everyone at the Lincoln County Courthouse wanted at least one copy of the bulletin. Some even wanted two. While I was making change for a lawyer waiting to try a case, Mr. Bowman, the county clerk, beckoned to me.

"Joe Wood?"

"Yes, sir?"

"I've heard you take on printing jobs, as well as publishing the newspaper. That right?"

"It is, sir," I answered. Printing for the county clerk's office could be a big job.

"We just got word from Augusta that the state legislature passed an act concerning the raising of volunteers for the war. They're promising printed copies, but not for another ten days. Could you print twenty-five copies before then? We'll need one for every town in Lincoln County, plus some to spare for the county officers."

"How long is the Act, sir?"

"About twenty pages. Short pages, though."

Twenty pages. A job that big would mean having the money to pay back Mr. Shuttersworth for sure! I wanted this job. I needed this job.

"Could I see a copy of the bill?"

"I won't be getting it 'til this afternoon. When it comes in, I'll send it down to you. Can you get me an answer then, as to how much it would cost, and how long it would take?"

"I'll let you know immediately," I assured him.

I hardly remember the rest of my walk through town. Twenty pages! I'd never done a job that large. Did I have enough paper in stock? Could I do the job fast enough? Printing wasn't what would take the time; it was typesetting that'd eat up hours.

I could hardly wait to get back to the office to check my paper supply and start making up some more ink.

I'd ask Owen if he'd help. Mixing ink was like Ma's making piecrusts: Even when you put together the exact same amounts of pine pitch, flaxseed oil, and lamp black—soot gathered from lamps and chimneys—and a trace of soap, the temperature of the room could change the result. Owen enjoyed the challenge. I suspected that was because making ink was messy, and he left for home or school proud of the blackened palms that proved he was working in our print shop.

I was figgering how much ink I'd be needing for the next week when I heard shouting down on Fore Street. It sounded like trouble. I ran the rest of the way.

Owen was in the middle of a group of boys, holding the few copies of the *Herald* he hadn't sold.

"My father's going to be a soldier," Owen was saying. "He's going to be a better soldier than anyone!"

"How can he be the best soldier when he's not white?" jeered Davy Searsmont.

"Yeah! My pa's going too, and he's the best with a musket in Lincoln County," said Liam Reynolds. "He can get a turkey or a deer or even a moose with just one shot!"

"There ain't gonna be any moose in South Carolina, Reynolds," said Davy. "So what are you and yer ma gonna eat when yer pa's off shootin' all them Southerners?"

"He'll kill 'em all, and get home in three months, jest like Mr. Lincoln says," said Liam. "He'll be home before the leaves fall."

"My father, too," put in Owen, strutting a little. "My father can kill any three Southerners, any time, faster'n your father!"

"Oh, yeah?" said Liam.

"Yeah!" said Owen.

Liam reached over and grabbed Owen's newspapers and threw them up in the air, scattering them all over the Custom House lawn. Owen's eyes followed them, but his feet didn't move. "My father'll be a better soldier than your father—any day."

"I'll bet your father doesn't even know how to shoot a musket. I've never seen him with one. Not once!" said Liam. "He's not even a real man. Real men are white!"

Owen's feet moved then. His left foot reached out and kicked Liam, hard, in his shins. But Liam's right hand was faster. It hit Owen's nose straight on. Owen's nose erupted in blood, spraying his own clothes and Liam's.

Liam moved back a step or two and reached up to touch his face. His hand came away covered with blood.

I stood back. If I stepped in, I'd be fighting Owen's battles for him. He'd never be able to show his face again. But I didn't want to see him hurt.

Then Davy and Liam and the other two boys took off.

It all happened so fast.

I ran toward Owen to make sure he was all right, but he just looked at me in embarrassment and ran toward his home.

I walked around the Custom House yard, picking up Owen's papers. The nasty words kept ringing in my ears. *Real men are white.*

This war wasn't just going to be fought in the South.

Chapter 23

Tuesday, April 16, afternoon

"Joe—there you are! I've got great news!"

Charlie was already back at the *Herald* office when I got there.

"First, I sold all of my share of *Herald*s." Charlie looked pointedly at those I was still carrying. I didn't tell him the copies were both mine and Owen's.

I put the extra papers on a shelf near the door and added my coins to those Charlie had already put on the desk. I couldn't get the picture of Owen's face, streaming with blood, out of my mind. Or, more important, the cruel words that had come before the blood.

I'd do the accounting later, after Owen had brought in the money he'd collected.

"I may have another printing job for us," Charlie continued. "Do you know Mr. Pendleton's ambrotype studio, near Bailey's Tavern?"

I nodded; of course I knew Mr. Pendleton's studio. When it opened six months ago, Mr. Pendleton had bought a few ads in the *Herald*. But not many in Wiscasset could afford having themselves immortalized using the new picture-taking machine; they'd sooner have their likenesses painted. An artist could paint them in color, in any size, and fix them up some—make them look the way they'd like to look. Mr. Pendleton's machine had no such sympathy.

"Mr. Pendleton's set up a flag as background in his studio, and says those going to war will want their pictures taken for their parents or wives or sweethearts. He wants to give each of his customers a card, two by four inches—something they can carry with them to list their name, company, state, hometown, and next of kin. He'd like us to print those up for him."

"Cards to keep themselves? Why?" I asked, without thinking.

"In case . . ." Charlie looked at me as though I were slow. "In case they get sick or wounded, or worse, and can't tell anyone who they are. So someone can write to their folks and tell them what happened." He stuck his hands into his trouser pockets, strode over to the window, and looked out onto the Green. Then he turned back to me. "Of course, I told him we'd print the cards."

"They would be simple to do," I agreed. "And we could get them done right away. This morning, in fact." I went to the desk where I kept my prices for card stock. "They would have to be on our heaviest paper. The stock we use for business or calling cards."

"He'll pay a decent price, I think," said Charlie. "There's no one else in Wiscasset who can do the job, and he wants the cards as soon as possible."

"I'll figger out how much we'd charge him. Then you can go back and tell him. I'd want to print them right away, since we may be getting in another job this afternoon."

"What's that?" Charlie asked.

"The county clerk's office is getting a copy of an act just passed in Augusta detailing the rules for recruiting and the laws governing the troops. It's twenty pages—longer than anything we've ever done. Even longer than Reverend Merrill's sermons. And they need it as soon as possible, to get a copy to every town in Lincoln County."

"Is there time to do that much?" Charlie asked. "What if there's more news? Even if we finish the cards for Mr. Pendleton this morning, there are only two of us. Maybe you may want to live your life in this office, but I don't."

Without Charlie I'd never be able to do the job for the county clerk. Charlie couldn't leave now.

"It's just a few days more, Charlie—I promise. And Owen will help. He's bright, and he's learning fast." I didn't mention what I'd seen that morning, but thought it might be good to keep Owen busy and away from the other restless boys until things calmed down.

"I don't know," Charlie said, shaking his head.

"Someone's going to bring a copy of the Act over from the county clerk's office this afternoon. We'll look at it then and decide," I said. "Why don't we take a break and have something to eat before we make any more decisions?"

We were halfway to the Mansion House kitchen, where Charlie planned to entice Mrs. Giles into finding us something tasty for dinner, when Reverend Merrill stopped us.

"I was coming to look for you boys. I'm in need of your assistance."

"Yes, Reverend," I answered, hoping it wouldn't take too long. My stomach was beginning to growl. I remembered I hadn't eaten breakfast.

"I was just up at the courthouse. The officers of the court have called a town meeting at four o'clock this afternoon at Wawenock Hall to share news from Augusta regarding President Lincoln's request for troops. There's no time for you to print a broadside, but I've already handwritten a notice and posted it in Mr. Johnston's store. I'll go to the taverns and other establishments and post notices there. Would you boys go to the waterfront stores and to homes where people may have gathered, and spread the word? It's critical that as many of our citizens as possible, of all ages, attend this afternoon's meeting."

Charlie and I looked at each other.

"Of course," said the reverend, "I assume you'll be covering the meeting for the *Herald,* and the county clerk said you'd be printing up the bill we'll be discussing, too."

"We will," I said. I looked over at Charlie. "It's our patriotic duty, Reverend."

"And you'll be paid well, I'm sure," Reverend Merrill said. "Just spread the word as best you can." He pulled his cloak around him and hurried down the hill toward Water Street.

"He acted as though we were messenger boys," said Charlie, looking after him. "Let's at least stop and get some bread first."

"Someone has to let people know. He needs folks who are reliable, and we are," I said, proudly. "But I sure wouldn't mind having something to chew on as we talk to folks."

"I wonder why the meeting has to be held so quickly," said Charlie as we headed inside the Mansion House kitchen. "Why couldn't they have waited until tomorrow? Farmers and others who live outside town won't hear the news soon enough to get to the church by four o'clock."

"That's why we'll be taking very good notes this afternoon," I answered, filling my pockets with anadama bread. "And not getting much sleep tonight. It looks like we'll be setting another issue of the paper, along with the text of that Maine State Act."

More money toward what I owed Mr. Shuttersworth.

Chapter 24

Tuesday, April 16, 4:00 p.m.

Word about the town meeting spread further and faster than I'd imagined possible.

By three-thirty Wawenock Hall was more than half full. By three forty-five the news that a meeting was about to be held was ringing from the church steeple. That bell was the object of local pride, as it had been made by Paul Revere, who'd earned recognition for actions other than his casting of bells. What would old Paul think of the situation our country had gotten itself into today?

Charlie and I perched on the edge of our seats in the first row of the balcony, where we could see everyone who came in. Ma and Pa had closed our store for the occasion. Owen and his parents were in the second row, and Charlie's father was there, too. I saw Miss Averill from the telegraph office, and old Mrs. Sayward hobbling in on two canes. Everyone in town seemed to have come.

To no one's surprise, Captain Tucker and Reverend Merrill took seats on the dais, which was hung with five of the largest Stars and Stripes I'd ever seen. Perhaps they'd been used for Fourth of July celebrations and tucked away in private attics. The room practically smelled of patriotism.

You understand, I suppose, that Wiscasset doesn't have a mayor. Decisions about town matters are made, as in most New England communities, based on majority votes at town meetings, or by the selectmen, who are elected at those town meetings. Special meetings like this one are chaired either by the reverend, by virtue of his relationship with the Almighty, or by Captain Tucker, because he was chairman of the selectmen, or, as some would say behind his back, by virtue of his relationship with the almighty dollar. They were both present this afternoon, as was the county clerk, since Wiscasset held the distinction of being the seat of Lincoln County.

I pulled out my notebook.

At 4 p.m. Captain Tucker stood and gave a spirited and patriotic speech to give expression to Wiscasset's loyalty and attachment to the Constitution and the Union. He then announced that 2,500 volunteers from Massachusetts were already quartered in Boston's Faneuil Hall, awaiting orders.

The crowd murmured, loudly. Captain Tucker certainly had their attention with *that* news. Maine had been part of Massachusetts until 1820, and competition was still high between our two states. How had Massachusetts managed to organize their volunteers so quickly?

"Our country stands tonight in an awful dilemma, and what the result will be, to us and to our country's future, only God can tell. President Lincoln has asked for our help. You've probably also heard that our great State of Maine has no money to raise or pay troops. Well, I'm here to share the good news—that several of the largest banks in Portland have offered to fund our soldiers, and General Samuel Veazie, patriot, decorated veteran of the War of 1812, one of Maine's staunchest abolitionists, and owner of several lumber mills, as well as the Bangor and Old Town Railroad, has given $50,000 from his own pockets to aid in the efforts to raise volunteers. So, although the funding problem is not solved, it is well on its way to being settled." [Cheers from the audience!]

Tonight we welcome Mr. Edmund Bowman, Lincoln County clerk of courts, to explain what is being asked of us, as citizens of Maine, and of this great and free country of ours."

Mr. Bowman rose, cleared his throat, and read what I immediately realized must be the document he'd asked me to print. The Act to Raise Volunteers authorized the State of Maine to enlist, enroll, and muster ten regular regiments and three regiments of militia, each of up to a thousand men, into the service of the State of Maine, for two years.

I touched Charlie's arm and whispered, "Not three months, like Lincoln said, Charlie. Two years!" Charlie shook off my hand. He was listening to every word as if he were memorizing it.

When Mr. Bowman read that you had to be eighteen years old to volunteer, Charlie groaned softly.

Most of the rest of the document was clearly meant to reassure mothers and wives that their men would be in good hands away from home. Rules which stated that every soldier must attend divine services; could not use profanities; must not duel; could not sleep or drink while on duty; could not plunder; could not mutiny or desert; and could not leave his unit without permission, were all met by nods of approval throughout the hall.

After Mr. Bowman finished reading the document—which didn't sound as long as twenty pages, I thought; some of the pages must be very short—Captain Tucker rose again.

"Twenty-three hundred of us, from the youngest babe to the oldest great-grandmother, live here within the boundaries of Wiscasset. Among our number we hope to raise enough volunteers for one company—one hundred volunteers, within the next week—to leave immediately. Mr. Edwin Smith"—Captain Tucker gestured at Edwin, who was sitting in the front row—"has already agreed to head such a company. He'll take charge of recruiting men to serve with him in defense of our beloved country. As soon as he has his quota, he and his company will report to Rockland. From there, they will go wherever they are called to ensure that the Union we all so love shall be preserved."

There was great applause and cheering for Edwin Smith.

"Since only the good Lord knows where the fighting will be," Captain Tucker continued, "we will also be establishing a Home Guard, to consist of men too old and boys too young to be soldiers in the army, but who can defend us here at home. Plans for such a Home Guard are still being developed, but I plan to lead this effort, and have already applied to Augusta for cannons to defend Wiscasset, to be strategically placed in old Fort Edgecomb on Davis Island, which we will repair and make usable again."

Captain Tucker paused a moment. "This is a dark day in the history of our country. Only God knows what the future will bring, so it is most fitting that Reverend Merrill end this meeting with a prayer."

While Reverend Merrill was asking for divine guidance for the men of Wiscasset in making their decision about volunteering to defend the Stars and Stripes, and the freedom of us all, I couldn't help looking down at my friends and neighbors, most of whom had their heads bowed.

Who would be leaving and going to war?

Who would be coming back?

The world outside Wiscasset seemed all too near.

Chapter 25

I quoted Mr. Pendleton the sum of $5.00 to print one hundred identification cards for the soldiers, and Charlie went off to tell him. That would be a fast job: Not much type to set, and I'd checked; I had enough of the heavier card stock needed.

With that $5.00, I'd have $54.45. Only $10.50 to go! But it was already Tuesday, and the money was due next Monday. I needed that job printing the Act.

While Charlie was off talking with Mr. Pendleton, I spoke with Mr. Bowman, who agreed we could also print sections of the Act as an insert to the *Herald,* where we'd add details of how it was to be implemented locally.

By the time Charlie and I were both back at the *Herald* office, I'd decided to send Charlie home for the night.

"I'll get everything organized so we can print the cards first thing in the morning, and start setting type for the Act," I told him. "If we're fresh then, we'll be able to work through tomorrow, except that I'll have to take an hour or so off in the afternoon. I promised my parents I'd watch the store. By that time we'll all need a little time off."

Since Charlie was still convinced Nell was a fraud, I didn't want him to know that Ma and Pa were going to consult her. That was our family's business, not Charlie's, although I knew he'd probably find out somehow. Wiscasset was a small town. Few people could keep secrets here.

Charlie nodded. "I can deliver the cards while you're at the store."

"Good plan," I agreed. I kept thinking of the $5.00 Mr. Pendleton had agreed to pay. I wanted those cards finished and the money in my box before he changed his mind. "I'll stop and fetch Owen on my way to the office," I added. "I'll be here by six-thirty tomorrow morning. Sharp."

"I'll check at the telegraph office," Charlie volunteered, "to make sure nothing happened down south overnight."

"Agreed."

"See you tomorrow," said Charlie, pulling on his jacket. "I'm curious to hear what people are saying about this afternoon's meeting. Travelers may not be interested in local details, but some Wiscasset men come to drink in the Mansion House tavern. I suspect there'll be some interesting talk tonight."

"I wonder who'll volunteer." I wondered out loud. "Captain Tucker said we need one hundred men. One hundred!"

"We should be finding out soon enough," said Charlie. "Good night!"

As I'd anticipated, it only took me an hour to set the type for the soldier's identification card. I hated thinking of what such cards might be used for, but was careful to make them large enough to inscribe with the information needed, and small enough to put in a pocket. I wished there was some way to keep them from smearing in the rain, but all ink smeared. Soldiers would have to wrap their cards in cloth or leather.

It was dark by the time I left the office and walked slowly toward home.

What would families do when their men were gone? What would the town do? Men farmed the land, ran the stores, and fished the rivers. They were pharmacists and smithies, shipbuilders and ministers, like Reverend Merrill. They were doctors and lawyers. How could these men just leave and turn into soldiers?

For a few young men, like Edwin Smith—who'd finished his time at Bowdoin College and hadn't yet married or opened his law practice—it might make sense to go. But there weren't a hundred Edwin Smiths in Wiscasset.

Our kitchen was warm and smelled of baked apples and cinnamon. Ma was pulling a hot dried-apple pie out of the oven, and Pa had gotten his Bible down off the shelf in the corner of the kitchen where it always sat. Trusty wagged his tail in happiness at my arrival.

Pa never read the Bible unless it was Sunday.

"Mmm!" I said. "Apple pie! What's the occasion?"

"I put the pie in before we closed up the store and went to that meeting," said Ma. "I hoped you'd be coming back here soon so we could all eat together. With the world moving so fast these days, we've hardly seen you in the past week."

"Sorry. I have to get up early tomorrow, too. I've been asked to print copies of that Act Mr. Bowman read from—enough copies for every town in the county." I sat down at the table. Pa moved the Bible to one side and Ma started cutting large slices of her pie. "But I haven't forgotten I'm to be here to watch the store for you tomorrow, while you talk with Miss Gramercy. What time is that?"

"One o'clock," said Pa. "We appreciate your taking the time, son. I expect we'll be getting many customers tomorrow, as people start thinking about what was talked about today at the meeting, and making their decisions."

"Who do you think'll go to soldiering?" I asked, filling my mouth with crisp crust and sweet apple filling. "It's a big decision, to sign up to fight, and be gone two years."

"Thank goodness you're too young to be thinking about it for yourself, son," said Ma. "Eighteen is still young to be going. I'd hate to be the mother of one of the boys who sign up."

"No; I'm not thinkin' that way," I said. "I love my country, but soldierin' isn't for me. I'm good with words and accounts. I have the newspaper to run here, and I can help you and Pa with the store. In war, people will want news, and they'll need provisions. There'll be plenty for me to do in Wiscasset. And Captain Tucker said he was settin' up that Home Guard. I'll ask if I can help with that. I suspect I can make more difference here in Wiscasset than I could as one more soldier on a battlefield."

She smiled. "I'm glad you're thinking that way, Joe. After losing your brother, I don't want to lose you, too. Tonight I suspect a lot of boys in town are aching to go and be heroes."

"Could be. Charlie would like to go, I think, but he's not eighteen, so Wiscasset's stuck with him, too," I said.

Ma looked over at Pa, who'd been quiet the whole time. "You want to say something, Abiel?"

"Son, sounds like you and Charlie'll be taking real good care of Wiscasset during this war we've gotten ourselves into," said Pa, in a low voice.

I looked at him. "Not everyone's leavin', Pa. Charlie and I won't be the only ones here."

"Well, now, that's true. But I want you to know, I believe you're going to do a darn good job of it all. You're close to a man now, and I trust you with everything I hold dear in my life."

"Pa?"

"That's why. . ." Pa looked over at Ma, and reached his hand out to grasp hers. "That's why I've decided that tomorrow, I'm going to enlist."

"Pa—no! We need you here! What if . . ."

I looked from Pa to Ma and back again. I couldn't say the words.

"I'll be home just as soon as Mr. Lincoln is sure we've got the job done. You know us Mainers, Joe; we're reliable. When our country needs us, we go."

I couldn't say anything. Didn't he think his family needed him, too? Was his country more important than Ma and me?

"You'll be fine. You'll be the man of the house when I'm gone. I trust you to take care of your ma. Watch out for her, and make sure she doesn't work too hard at the store."

Ma had tears in her eyes.

"Why, Catherine, you'll both be so busy, you won't even know I'm gone."

"We'll know you're gone, Abiel. We'll know," said Ma.

How could he leave? Just when everything at home seemed so much better?

I banged my fork down on the table, ran upstairs, and slammed the door of my room. Hard. How could Pa desert us?

Even if I could pay Mr. Shuttersworth his money, there was no way I could run a printing business and help Ma with the store, too.

It wasn't fair. I hated this war, and I hated what Pa was doing.

Chapter 26

Wednesday, April 17, morning

Perhaps God wanted to remind us mud season hadn't ended yet.

Heavy rain drilling on the low roof over my head woke me in the dark morning. I pulled Ma's soft quilt over my head. Why should I get up in the cold and dank and work long hours? With Pa enlisting, I'd never be able to keep the *Herald* going, even if I *did* manage to pay back Mr. Shuttersworth.

I buried my head further under the covers.

But rain meant little to Trusty. "No, Trusty—not today!" Seeing me move, he'd jumped up on the bed and pulled the quilt down, hoping for a game.

I dragged myself out of bed and pulled on my trousers and a warm shirt and jacket. It might be halfway through April, but warm weather had not yet reached the coast of Maine.

Ma had already set the kettle on to boil. One benefit of having a store in the family was always having both coffee and tea at hand. She handed me a mug of steaming coffee. It smelled bracing, but was too hot to drink. I sat down at the table.

"Where's Pa?"

"He's already gone to talk with young Mr. Smith about the enlistment," said Ma, pouring hot tea from the teapot into a cup for herself. "He wanted to be one of the first to sign up."

"He's really going to do it, then. Enlist."

"He is." Ma stirred her cup of tea hard and fast, as though she were mixing biscuits. "He won't be deterred. Your pa's a stubborn man." Her lips were taut. "And a patriot."

I put the coffee down. My stomach was beginning to knot, but I couldn't complain to Ma. She'd bear most of the burden in Pa's absence. "We'll be fine, Ma. I'll take good care of you."

Ma smiled. "You will . . . and I of you. And we'll write to your pa and keep in touch. President Lincoln said the war might only be a few months. Let's hope he's right."

I nodded.

"There's a small piece of pie left from dinner. I saved it for you." Ma fetched the pie from the pantry. Pie was a common breakfast in Maine, and apple, one of my favorites. And, for all of my thoughts, I was hungry.

"I'll be back before one o'clock," I said.

"Thank you. We'll see you then." Ma looked at me, straight this time. "Don't you be worrying, Joe. You and I'll make it just fine. We will. Your pa has to do this, for our country. And for himself."

"I understand that's what he says; I just don't know why it has to be him. Why it can't be someone without a wife, or a son. Without responsibilities."

Ma shook her head. "There's few without such. In war, all must sacrifice. Our sacrifice is your father." She turned, and I could see her tears starting. "Now, you go on. Go to the newspaper office, and print up the words for the other towns, so folks there will know what we in Wiscasset found out yesterday. They need to know, too. That's your job. Be off with you."

The last of the pie stuck in my throat, but I headed out, holding my jacket tight around me and trying not to step in the deepest puddles.

My first stop was the Bascombs' house, to get Owen. I'd need all the help I could get today.

"Good morning, Joe," Mr. Bascomb said, as he answered my knock. "I assume you're looking for Owen this dreadful morning?"

"I could use his help over at the *Herald* office, sir. We're setting type for the state's Act to Raise Volunteers."

Owen slid in front of his father. "I can be ready in a minute, Joe. I can go, can't I, Father?"

"Get your jacket on first." His father looked down. "And your shoes. And get some bread and meat from your mother. You haven't had breakfast yet."

Owen disappeared in the direction of the kitchen.

"Owen does love being with you and Charlie. It's good of you to find work that a boy his age can do without his making a nuisance of himself."

"He's no nuisance, Mr. Bascomb. Owen's a big help. He's learned a lot about setting type and printing. When I've got a big job, like today, I really need his help."

"That's good then; I'm glad. Sometimes I worry he's in the way down there. He can be clumsy and awkward. Did you see the bloody nose he got running into a tree the other day?"

Owen must not have told his father about that gang of boys. I wouldn't have told my pa either. Luckily I didn't have to say anything because Owen appeared, shoes and jacket on, his brightly colored parrot on his head. "Can I bring Gilthead with me today?"

"Not today, Owen," I said. "He'll want to fly about, and you know he makes messes. We're going to have papers all over the room. We have too much to do to clean up after him today."

Owen looked down. "He wouldn't be a bother. I'd clean up after him."

"Joe said no, boy," said his father. "Now go and put Gilthead back in his cage. That bird has too much freedom as it is." He shook his head. "Ever since Owen's uncle brought that parrot back from Cuba, the bird's been nothing but trouble. The boy does love him, though."

Mr. Bascomb turned back to me. "So, you're printing up the Act to Raise Volunteers, eh? What do you think: Will Wiscasset be able to get one hundred men to volunteer?"

"I don't know." I hesitated. "But my pa's going to sign up."

"Then I'll be seeing him at Edwin Smith's home. I'm volunteering, too," said Mr. Bascomb. "It's a man's duty to defend his country and keep it free for his children and grandchildren. I want Owen to grow up in a country where he can travel to any state and live and do business without fear. That's why I'll be fighting. I'm guessing your pa will be fighting for the same reasons. This country is called the *United* States for a reason. We need to stick together—not be torn apart."

Owen was back, this time with a hunk of bread and some meat in his hand and no Gilthead. "I'm ready to go. I can eat this on the way."

"Good luck, Mr. Bascomb," I said. "We'll be working until a little past twelve, and then takin' a break. Owen will be able to come home for nooning. Then we'll go back and work through the afternoon."

Owen and I had the press ready to print the identification cards and the font trays lined up to begin setting the Act by the time Charlie burst through the door.

"News!" Charlie said, tossing his sodden jacket and hat on the floor, as usual. "Virginia has seceded!"

"Succeeded in doing what?" asked Owen, who was carefully inking the press under my supervision.

"Not succeeded, you goose! *Seceded!* They've decided they're not staying with the Union—the Northern states. They're going with the states in the South," said Charlie. "It just came in on the wires. They're the eighth state to leave the Union. And Virginia is right next to Washington, where President Lincoln lives."

"How many states are on our side?" asked Owen.

I counted on my fingers. "Twenty-eight, I think."

"Then we'll win," said Owen, confidently. "There are more of us. And"—he stood very tall—"my father is going to be a soldier. He's going to enlist this morning."

"I wish my father would enlist," Charlie burst out. "He says he's too old, and that I need him here. He keeps saying he's the only family I've got. But I'm almost a man. I think it's just an excuse. I don't think he wants to go. Maybe he's scared. I told him that, too."

"Maybe he's thinking of you, Charlie," I said. "I wish my pa wouldn't go."

"Your pa?" said Charlie, turning to look at me. "Your pa's enlisting, too?"

"He went this morning, like Owen's father."

"Your father's older than mine! See? My father *is* just looking for an excuse! And I'm going to tell him so, next time I see him." Charlie slammed his hand against the wall. "If only I were eighteen, I'd sign those papers in a minute. I wouldn't even think twice about it."

"We're not getting anything done here," I said. "Let's get started. Charlie, you operate the press for the identification cards while I start setting the type for the Act. After you finish printing the cards, you can work on the Rules Governing Troops, for the second column. We'll work until about twelve-thirty, then I'll go home and mind the store so Ma and Pa can keep their appointment. While I'm doing that, both of you can get something to eat and check the telegraph again before we meet back here this afternoon."

"Then I'll write up a box about Virginia seceding," said Charlie.

"Good idea," I agreed. "We'll put that on the front page of the *Herald*—maybe even at the top. It'll show how important it is that people enlist as soon as possible. But let's get the cards printed first."

"You go ahead and work on that," said Charlie. "I'm going to talk to my father again. I'm going to tell him both your fathers are enlisting. Maybe that will make him feel like he should enlist, too!"

He grabbed his jacket from the floor and raced out, not even stopping to shut the door.

Chapter 27

"You're certain you can handle the store yourself?" Pa asked.

Hadn't he noticed that since Ethan's death I'd often been left in charge of the store?

"He'll be fine, dear." Ma adjusted her best bonnet and lace wrap. The way she dressed advertised the latest offerings we had for sale.

"When Charlie and I interviewed Miss Gramercy on Monday, she said a spirit only communicated with her when there was a message to be delivered. Maybe Ethan said everything he needed to the last time he spoke to you, Pa," I said. They were so excited about their meeting; I didn't want them to be disappointed.

"I hope she'll hear something," said Ma. "But even if she doesn't, we'll know we tried to tell Ethan how much we love him and miss him. How much we thank him for coming back to us for that brief moment when he did speak through Miss Gramercy." Ma was now pulling on her best silk-lined kidskin gloves. "The idea of being able to communicate with Ethan is so very exciting. I'm glad your father was able to reserve a session for us." She gave Pa a special smile.

"We won't be long, now, Joe," Pa reminded me, as though I were Owen's age. He straightened his waistcoat once more. "We reserved a forty-minute session, so we should be back in an hour, should anyone need our help in the store."

"I'll be fine," I repeated. Then I asked, "Pa, did you do it this morning? Did you enlist?"

"I did as I said I would, son." Pa looked at me proudly. "I'll be in the first group to march out of Wiscasset to fight for our Stars and Stripes."

The door closed after them.

I walked through the shop as I had thousands of times, straightening the items for sale. I could have done it blindfolded.

One whole corner was filled with sewing supplies: Needles for knitting and plain sewing and fancywork; threads and buttons of all kinds. Stacked bolts of flowery spring fabric were arranged to appeal to women thinking of warm days to come.

Another corner was filled with mourning goods: black and purple fabrics and threads; ready-made mourning hats for both men and women; black capes and gloves; black-bordered handkerchiefs for the bereaved; and black-bordered envelopes and stationery, so sad news could be conveyed appropriately. Ma also stocked pins, lockets, and rings designed to hold strands of the deceased's hair that could be braided and arranged carefully, perhaps in the shape of a lily or other mourning flower, and kept as a remembrance. Wide black ribbons and wreaths were designed to hang on front doors to let others know the occupants of a house had lost someone dear to them. There was even a box of glass vials to hold tears shed in memory of a lost loved one. Death was a part of life. This section of the store was one of our most profitable.

I re-wound black ribbons that had loosened from their rolls. Many customers who'd bought items from this section were now asking Nell Gramercy to contact those they'd lost. Was paying Nell for her services any different than their buying mourning jewelry? How many people in town would be coming here to buy mourning apparel after losing a husband or father in this war? I thought of Pa, and Mr. Bascomb, and Edwin Smith.

The shop bell broke my thoughts. It was Charlie.

"Why are you here?" I asked. "You didn't come back to the office. Owen and I have finished the cards for Mr. Pendleton. I thought you were going to deliver the cards, and then write the article about Virginia seceding and set type for the Act."

"I thought I'd keep you company for a while," he answered.

"I'm not lonely. I wish I could have gone with my folks." I finally decided to tell Charlie where my parents were. "They reserved a private session with Nell Gramercy. I'd like to hear what—if anything—Ethan might say, but someone had to mind the store." I didn't tell Charlie Ma and Pa hadn't asked if I'd like to go with them.

"They're paying money for that? Nell was just lucky the first time, to say something significant to your father. Most likely it won't happen again," said Charlie.

"Part of me's afeared Ma and Pa will be disappointed," I admitted.

"And lose their money," Charlie pointed out. "How much is she charging for a private session?"

"I didn't ask. But Pa said it was hard to schedule a time. Many people in town want to talk with her."

"I'll bet she's making a small fortune," Charlie said. "I suspect the war is adding to her coffers. How do you think she and her aunt and uncle paid for those fancy clothes they're wearing?" He walked toward a part of the shop concealed by a rose-colored velvet curtain.

"Charlie, get away from that corner! You know you're not supposed to go over there."

"No one else is here this afternoon. What harm would it do to look? You work here, and it hasn't done you any grave moral damage."

I moved over in front of the curtain and crossed my arms. "I'm in charge of the shop, and I don't want anyone to come in and see you behind there. It's indecent. No boys or men are allowed in there except Pa and me, and that's only because we work here. Most of the time Ma handles that department herself."

Charlie made a motion as if to part the curtain, but then backed off. "All right, all right. Relax. I've seen corsets and stockings and petticoats and drawers before. They hang on the laundry line at the Mansion House every day. I was just teasing."

I kept my eyes on him. Charlie couldn't always be trusted when he had mischief on his mind. "You'd be a big help to me if you'd go back to the office, get the cards we printed, and deliver them to Mr. Pendleton. Owen should be back any minute. One of us should be in the office when he's working, in case he has questions."

"All right! But setting type hour after hour is boring. You have an hour off; I needed to stretch my legs a little."

I bit my tongue. Charlie'd taken the whole morning off so far as I could tell. But, then, it wasn't his print shop. "I'll be at the office as soon as my parents get back."

He'd only been gone a few minutes when Mrs. Parsons came in to buy a bonnet for her niece in Camden. She spent fifteen minutes debating whether a pink hat with white flowers looked better than a white

138

hat with pink flowers. She bought a yellow bonnet with ribbons instead of either of them.

Then Mr. Chase stopped by to see if Pa would usher at the Congregational Church on Sunday morning, and Widow Quinn bought some red silk embroidery floss for a cushion she was stitching for her sister's parlor.

When the bell on the shop door jingled again it was Ma and Pa. I gave Pa the message from Mr. Chase and then asked, "Was Miss Gramercy able to contact Ethan?"

Ma's smile answered. "She did! And he sent you a message."

"Me!"

"He said he missed his little brother Joe, but that you had work yet to do in life. He would see you again someday, when your work was finished."

"He wished us all well," added Pa, "and said he had no pain where he was—only joy. That the next world was not to be feared."

"It made me shiver, hearing that girl talk," said Ma, putting her outside bonnet carefully under the counter and replacing it with the one she wore inside. "I'm so glad we were able to arrange a time with her."

"Nell Gramercy's gift is a true one," said Pa. "We're blessed she chose to share it with us in Wiscasset."

"I have to get back to the *Herald* office," I said, patting Trusty on his head. "I'm glad the meeting went well." I hugged Ma, and then I hugged Pa, too. How long would it be before I wouldn't be able to do that?

To my surprise, Charlie was alone in the office.

"Where's Owen?"

"Don't know. He hasn't been here," he said. "I took the cards to Mr. Pendleton, and he gave me the five dollars right off. The money's in the desk." Charlie gestured to where I put any paper money we earned. "For someone who wants to learn the business, Owen seems to have disappeared." Charlie slammed a font tray down on the table. "The day we need him most."

I didn't answer. Owen had been with me all morning; Charlie hadn't.

"I'm glad you're here," I said.

"I've been looking at the Act. It's printed on twenty pages now, but I think with smaller fonts, we can do it on ten. It's going to be ten full pages, though, and we've only just started the first." Charlie looked at me.

I nodded. "You're right. We're going to take four of the pages and distribute them, with one or two boxed items, like one for the news from Virginia, as an issue of the *Herald*. That will mean we don't have to print the *Herald* in addition to printing the Act. But it's still going to be a lot of work."

"Do we even have enough pieces of type?"

I shook my head. "We'll have to set two pages, print them, then set another two pages. We have no choice."

Charlie whistled. "Godfrey mighty. When does all of this have to be done?"

"First thing Monday morning. At the latest."

Charlie shook his head. "I do like that we're among the first to know what's happening with the war. Some boys our age don't even understand what's happening. But to get all that typesetting and print-ing done, we'll hardly be able to sleep from now until Monday."

"You're right. Without both of us, the job can't be finished." I hoped Charlie wouldn't think of an excuse to be somewhere else, as he sometimes did when there was work to be done.

"Then why are you talking instead of setting type?" Charlie handed me a type tray. "I stopped at the telegraph office on my way back from Mr. Pendleton's. There's no news to concern ourselves with for the moment—although the Sixth Massachusetts has left Boston for Washington."

"While we're still recruiting here in Maine. I wonder how many men have gone to Edwin Smith's house to enlist today."

"And how long it'll take him to get his quota," Charlie said, setting pieces of type on the table. "Captain Tucker said one hundred men, but that's a lot for a town the size of Wiscasset." He reached to set another line.

"What did Mr. Pendleton say when you left the cards we printed with him? Is he getting much call for portraits?"

"I almost forgot. He wants to put an advertisement in the *Herald* this week, reminding families of his services. He was pleased with the cards. We only spoke briefly; two families were in his office, inquiring about appointments. One man wanted a portrait of his promised lady to carry with him. She was sniffling and crying and was all upset." Charlie's fingers were flying over the type.

Would Pa want to take a picture of Ma with him when he left? I'd saved out one of the cards for him. What if he were hurt somewhere, and no one nearby knew who he was? I'd make sure Pa filled it out and took it with him. Just in case.

We were interrupted by heavy steps on the stairs leading to the office, and then, a knock.

"Mr. Bascomb!" Charlie said, opening the door. "What brings you here this afternoon?"

"I came to talk with Owen," Mr. Bascomb said, looking around the room.

"Owen isn't here," I said. "He left about twelve-thirty and hasn't been back. We assumed he went home to you."

Mr. Bascomb frowned. "He was home, sure enough, but I had to give him some upsetting news, and he ran out. I assumed he'd come here. If he's not here, then I don't know where he is."

"If you don't mind my asking, what was he upset about?"

For a moment, Mr. Bascomb was silent. Then he spoke slowly, saying each word distinctly, as though to ensure his words were understood.

"I went this morning to enlist. To serve my country, as a man should." His mustache quivered with emotion. "Captain Smith turned me down flat. Said they weren't taking no men of color in the Union Army. Didn't matter who I was, or how long I'd known everyone else in line, or what I could do. Said I couldn't serve in the Army alongside white folks. Said that was the rule come down from Washington, set in 1820. Didn't matter that men of my color served in the Revolutionary War, and are serving now in the Navy."

Mr. Bascomb headed toward the door, then turned around.

"I don't blame my boy for being upset, but I want him home— where we can talk about it together. If you see him, you tell him that. And you tell him I'm still proud to be an American, and he should be too. No matter what those people in Washington say."

Chapter 28

Charlie'd left the newspaper office at suppertime, but I'd stayed until the oil in my lamp had burned out and my eyes were too tired to set any more type. I'd slept a few hours at home, and was having bread and cold meat for breakfast before heading back, when someone pounded on our kitchen door.

Pa opened it.

"John—good morning! What brings you here so early? The sun's barely up."

It was Mr. Bascomb.

"My Owen didn't come home last night," said Mr. Bascomb. "I thought maybe he was at your place. Or that Joe might have an idea of where he'd be."

I got up from the table. "I haven't seen Owen since yesterday morning, and he hasn't been here. But I'll help you look." I started putting on my jacket.

"How long's he been missing for?" asked Pa, reaching for his own coat.

"Since a little past one o'clock yesterday afternoon," Mr. Bascomb replied. "I've looked everywhere. My wife's been crying the night through, making herself sick. In her condition, I don't know whether to worry more about her or the boy."

"Has he done anything like this before?" asked Pa.

"Never! He's a good boy. Works with your Joe and Charlie at the print shop instead of going to school some days, but that's no secret."

"Maybe he's with a friend," suggested Pa.

"He doesn't have any close friends that I know of, except for Joe and Charlie," said Mr. Bascomb. "Of course, no father knows everything about their children. What do you think, Joe? Where could he be?"

"I don't think he'd be with any other boys." I hesitated, wondering how much I should say about what I'd seen Monday. "He got into a fight the other day with some boys about his own age. He was real proud of you, Mr. Bascomb. He was bragging what a good soldier you were going to be. Some of the other boys were saying . . . nasty things."

"So that's how he got that black eye and nosebleed. I thought his story about running into a tree sounded suspicious. And then for him to hear what happened yesterday," Mr. Bascomb said, shaking his head in anger. "A boy shouldn't have to take on the battles of grown men."

"Joe told me what happened when you went to enlist," said Pa. "It's neither fair nor right, John. The army needs men like you. The decision out of Washington must have something to do with that slavery issue down south."

"They're saying it's because Lincoln doesn't want to aggravate the slave-holding states that haven't left the Union. But don't fool yourself—they're afraid white men even here in the North won't want to serve alongside men of color, to sleep in the same tents and use the same latrines. And too many folk think men of my color won't make good soldiers. Don't forget: Nathaniel Gordon, a Maine man, is sitting in a New York prison, accused of engaging in the slave trade in West Africa last summer. But today that's neither here nor there. Today I'd appreciate your help in finding my Owen and bringing him home."

Pa nodded. "One thing's for sure: If he's been hiding since yesterday afternoon, he's raging hungry by now. I'd think he'd be coming home anytime."

"That's what I kept thinking all night. That it was cold, and he'd be hungry. I figure he's either somewhere with a friend, or something's happened to him. Something bad," said Mr. Bascomb.

"We're going to find him," I said. "I'll get Charlie; he'll look, too."

"I'd planned to check with the businesses down on Water Street next," said Mr. Bascomb. "They've been closed all night. Now that they're opening, someone might find him if he was hiding there."

"I'll go out to the steam mill and then check the shipyards on Fore Street," said Pa. "Joe, after you get Charlie, why don't you boys head up Federal Street? Maybe one of the houses north of Main Street is vacant, or has a barn or shed Owen might hide in."

Where could Owen be? Was he hurt and alone somewhere? No one mentioned the one fear we all shared: the river.

Where Ethan had disappeared.

Chapter 29

"I told Father that Owen was missing. He said he'd check inside the inn, but I don't think Owen would be here. Besides, people would remember seeing a small boy," Charlie pointed out. "Although I suppose he might have hidden in one of the outbuildings. We'll look there."

The stable seemed a good place to start. Charlie checked the hayloft, while I looked in the stalls and in every guest's wagon or carriage.

"If Owen were looking for a place to hide, there are lots of places in here," I said. "Under the seats, and in the compartments for trunks, and under the hay. And there are several empty stalls." We called his name, but there was no answer. Old Mr. McKinley, who was in charge of the Mansion House stable, said he hadn't seen any boys.

We walked past Mr. Stacy's house and Mr. Turner's; no places there for a boy to hide.

The old burying ground had been filled long ago, and some of the worn granite headstones had toppled over. Wealthier families in town had moved their family members' bodies to the newer, more stylish, cemetery over on Spruce Point, where there was more space. Boys sometimes dared each other to climb the iron fence and explore the ancient graveyard. Owen wouldn't have gone in alone; Charlie and I were sure of that.

We continued down Federal Street, asking everyone we saw if they'd seen Owen. No one had. We walked all the way out of town until we came to the old granite jail.

"Mr. Cunningham is in there now, I guess," I said, looking at the small windows covered with iron bars.

"That'll show anyone who talks against the Union," said Charlie.

"Talking's one thing," I pointed out. "Refusing to do your job for the country's another. He wasn't jailed for talking."

"Guess not," admitted Charlie. He looked down the road, where it became more pitted and muddy. "Owen wouldn't have gone any farther than here, would he?"

I shook my head. "It's just farms out there on the Alna Road. Owen doesn't know anyone who lives that far from town. Let's go back."

We turned, neither of us saying anything for a long time.

Finally Charlie spoke. "Chances are he'll have turned up by the time we get back, don't you think? Wherever he was, probably he got hungry or thirsty and decided to go home."

"I hope so," I said. "He was so proud his father was going to be a soldier. And then, to have to face everyone he bragged to, after his father was turned down . . . That's got to be hard, Charlie. Mighty hard."

"I guess," said Charlie. "But he's young. He'll learn to live with it."

"Did your father change his mind after you talked with him yesterday? Is he enlisting?" I asked.

"Nah. He says he's too old, and can't shoot, and he's not interested in the politics of it all." Charlie dragged his foot, making a line in the dirt street. "Now *that's* embarrassing. He didn't even try to enlist."

"I wish my pa wasn't going," I said softly.

Charlie stopped. "What?"

"I know—it's patriotic and all. But I wish he'd let someone else go so he could stay home and help Ma with the store."

"But you must be so proud! I wish he were *my* pa!" Charlie laughed. "You have all the luck!"

"Luck? My brother died, and now Pa's leaving too; who knows if he'll be comin' back. And in the meantime, Ma has to run the store. Even if we get the Act printed in time to earn enough money so I can pay Mr. Shuttersworth, I'll be torn between helping her and running the *Herald*, never knowing what's happening to Pa." I took a few steps toward Charlie. "You're right. I'm lucky. Just plumb lucky."

I should have gone to the *Herald* office, or to the Bascombs' house to see if Owen had come home, but at that moment I was convinced I'd never get the printing job done, we'd never find Owen, and life would never work out the way I'd hoped it would.

And not even my best friend understood.

I left Charlie standing by the town water pump and headed home.

Chapter 30

"Did you find Owen?" Ma asked. "I've been worried about that boy all morning."

"Charlie and I didn't. Maybe someone else did."

Ma looked at me. "I would have been out there myself, but I've been kept busy all morning, selling goods and taking orders from women whose husbands and sons have enlisted." Her lips smiled, but her eyes didn't. "These are difficult days for everyone." She wiped her hands on her apron. "Your pa is still out looking, so far as I know. A lot of townsfolk are."

"Owen should have come home by now, Ma."

"If he were able." She glanced toward the corner of the kitchen where she'd hung a framed sketch an itinerant artist had drawn of Ethan when he was a toddler.

I hugged her. I was now taller than she was, I realized.

Many of the men in town had also gone out to look for Ethan. But his skiff had been missing too, so they'd known where to start the search. With Owen there were no such hints.

"I keep thinking of Owen's poor mother," said Ma. "After the store's closed today, I'll go sit with her. I have a loaf of cinnamon bread baking for her now."

Food. The way to console and show compassion.

"Your cinnamon bread's the best, Ma," I said. "Mrs. Bascomb will love it. And Owen, too, when he gets home."

We smiled at each other.

"I'm going down to the *Herald* office to check on things. Then I'll look for Owen again. Don't wait supper."

Ma nodded. "My thoughts and prayers go with you, and all the searchers."

Charlie was at the office, as I'd hoped. Neither of us mentioned our earlier talk.

"Owen's still missing," I said.

"I heard," Charlie answered. "People say they've looked everywhere. No one knows what to do, or where to look."

"Charlie, I've thought of someone who might be able to help us find Owen."

"Who? Everyone in town has already tried, Joe. Wiscasset isn't that big a place. There aren't that many places to look."

"We could ask Nell."

"What?"

"She could ask her spirits! Maybe Ethan, or some other spirit who knows Wiscasset, will have seen Owen."

"You want us to ask Nell Gramercy to holler up to all the ghosts around and see if any of them have seen Owen?" Charlie came over and put his hand on my forehead, as though testing me for fever.

I pushed him away. "Don't joke! What harm could it do to ask her? You've been wanting to test Nell, to see if her powers are real. Well, no one knows where Owen is, so no one would be able to tell her ahead of time, right? This would be a real test."

152

Charlie shook his head. "Her uncle would never let her do anything like that. Besides, she talks to people who've died. Owen hasn't died!"

"No, I don't believe Owen's dead," I agreed. I wasn't going to let myself believe that. Not yet. "He's probably hiding because he's mad that his father can't enlist. He's embarrassed because he bragged to the other boys about what a wonderful soldier his father would be."

"You're daft to even think of trying to involve Nell Gramercy."

"What harm would it do to ask her? She can say she can't do it— or doesn't want to do it," I said. "It'll be dark in a few hours. What if Owen's outside somewhere in the cold and wet? We need to do every- thing we can to find him."

"Nell Gramercy's a fake. You heard what that mariner said down at Bailey's. There's no reason to get her involved. If we try to see her, we'll just waste time we could be using to search, and we'll get in trou- ble with her uncle, and with my father, who's promised their family privacy. It's a crazy idea. I'll help you with printing; I'll look for Owen; but I won't get involved with a girl who says she hears voices."

"Does she eat in the Mansion House dining room?" I persisted. "Maybe we could talk to her there."

Charlie shook his head. "Her aunt and uncle have their meals and afternoon tea delivered to their rooms, and they're always together. Her room adjoins theirs. It won't work, Joe." He walked to the door of the office. "When you come to your senses and want to work on the printing, let me know. I'm going up to the Bascombs' house to see if any of the search groups need an extra man."

He slammed the door.

153

Uncertain Glory

I paced the floor. The unfinished trays of type we'd started to set for the Act sat accusingly on the table. I'd lost almost an entire day; I'd never get the job done now. But how could I sit here and set type when Owen's life might be in danger?

Appealing to Nell Gramercy might be crazy, but why not ask her? No one had been able to find Owen so far. Perhaps another set of eyes . . . or voices . . . would make a difference.

I had to try.

I sat down at the desk and wrote:

Dear Miss Gramercy,

Owen Bascomb, a young friend of mine, only nine years old, who works at the Herald, *has run away. He's been gone more than twenty-four hours now. His parents and everyone are real worried. If you and your voices could help find him and bring him home, I'd be most grateful. I'll be outside the* Mansion House *kitchen door after your tea.*

Sincerely yrs,

Joe Wood

I read it over, scratched out "Joe Wood" and wrote "Joseph Wood, owner, *Wiscasset Herald*." Then I added "P.S. This is not a trick, or for publication. I really need your help!"

I folded the letter and headed for the Mansion House.

Chapter 31

Thursday, April 18, midday

Mrs. Giles was bustling around the Mansion House kitchen, flour on her apron and hands, while tantalizing smells rose from the covered platters she was handing to Abby Tarbox and Rose Chambers, who were serving midday dinner to customers in the dining room.

"Joe Wood, whatever are you doing in my kitchen?" she asked, pushing me aside to reach for a plate of pastries. I hadn't been hungry before, but looking at those sweets made me feel like Trusty, his mouth open and dripping, waiting for me to give him a stew bone. "Charlie's not around," she added. "I haven't seen him since breakfast."

"I'm not looking for him," I said.

"Then get out of my way. I've a job to do," she said. "It's mealtime."

"Do you take a tea tray up to Nell Gramercy and the Allens?" I asked quickly, moving out of her way.

"I fix one for them," she said. "Rose is the one takes it up. Four-fifteen every afternoon, sharp. Why should that be a concern of yours?"

"Curious."

She stopped a moment, and eyed me. "Curious about that Miss Gramercy, I'd wager. Sweet little thing she is, even if she does have a strange way about her. Talking to the dead and all."

I nodded slightly. Whatever it took, to learn what I needed to know. I asked very softly, "Do you know her room number?"

She almost cackled. "I knew it! Young romance!"

Abby Tarbox tittered in the corner and winked at me. My cheeks turned as red as a courting cardinal.

"Guest-room numbers are strictly confidential," Mrs. Giles said, tossing some of her softest white rolls into a silver bowl and handing it to Abby. "Get this to table six, girl."

As soon as Abby had left the room, she turned to me. "Her room is number twenty-three, Joe. But if you tell anyone you heard it here, I'll box your ears, so help me. Now, get on with you. And don't get yourself or that girl in any trouble!"

I ran out the inside back door of the kitchen, the one that led to the wing where Charlie's room was. I could always say I was going to see him. I'd been in that corridor often enough, although those times, I'd been with Charlie. He'd once pointed out the narrow back staircase to the second and third floors—the one the maids used. I listened. Right now everyone seemed to be in the dining room.

I headed up. On the second floor a door opened to the hallway between the public rooms and the private rooms. Where room twenty-three would be.

The sound of dishes being served and people talking came from the dining room. I'd picked a good time.

Charlie had said that Nell and her family ate in her aunt and uncle's room. They were probably there now. My only chance was to slip my note under Nell's door and hope that she saw it before her uncle did.

Room 23, marked in large brass numbers, was on the left side of the hall.

I took the note out of my pocket, reached down, and slid it under the door—and felt a large hand grip my shoulder.

Chapter 32

Thursday, April 18, afternoon

Caught. But luckily, my note had already vanished under Nell's door.

"What are you doing here?"

It was Charlie's father. He'd seen me; there was no sense pretending.

"Leaving something for Miss Gramercy."

"Nothing that will annoy her, I hope." Mr. Farrar was a lot taller than Pa; I'd never noticed that before. "No, sir. A copy of the interview Charlie and I did with her." (Yup; I lied. But this was important, and I couldn't very well tell him the truth, could I?)

"And I suppose she told you this was her room?"

"How else would I have known?" I wasn't real good at looking innocent, but I did my best. I didn't want to get Mrs. Giles in trouble.

"Well, you've done what you came for; now get out of here."

I started down the hallway. Fast. Mr. Farrar's voice stopped me.

"Joe, where's Charlie? You two are usually together."

"He's out looking for Owen Bascomb."

"Ah, yes. No one's found that poor boy yet? Let's hope he turns up soon, and alive. You get on, and tell Charlie he's expected to check in here once in a while."

"Yes, sir. I'll tell him."

I scooted down the front stairs, between a few folks leaving the dining room. It was close to two-thirty, according to the grandfather clock in the lobby. If Nell were able to get away, it wouldn't be until after she'd had tea.

I had enough time to go home, get something to eat, and check in at the Bascombs' to see if Owen had shown up. I crossed my fingers that somehow he'd be there to greet me, and I could tell Nell I didn't need her voices after all. If I moved quickly I might even have time to set a few lines of type before coming back to the Mansion House.

I took off, running.

By a little past four-thirty I was back, outside the Mansion House kitchen door. I'd confirmed the news (or lack of it) all over town: No one had found a trace of Owen Bascomb. Men and boys had searched through sail lofts, boatyards, and lumberyards. Women and children had checked cellars, attics, ells, and barns. Storekeepers had checked that no one was hiding in their storerooms or under their counters or behind their cabinets. Even the tavern owners had hunted in their storage areas and kitchens. Owen had disappeared.

No one knew where else to look.

Except in the Sheepscot River. Now even its tidal flows seemed ominous. Mariners climbed down from wharves and docks and floats and checked the mudflats below. Gulls surveyed their search, hoping for tidbits of mussels or razor clams or crabs. But still, no trace of a missing nine-year-old boy.

Nothing.

Ominously, nothing.

Some people had already given up and gone home for the night.

"He'll show up, one way or the other," I heard one man say. "We have to get on with our lives."

I kept trying not to think about the day Ethan had disappeared. Maybe if we'd looked for him earlier. Or harder. Or more people had looked. Maybe . . .

We had to find Owen. How could we just stop looking?

I'd told no one about the note I'd left. It was enough that Charlie had laughed at me, and now Mrs. Giles thought I had a crush on Nell. My cheeks heated up at just the thought of that.

I stood in the shadows, behind the empty barrels stored by the kitchen entrance to the Mansion House, hoping Mrs. Giles wouldn't come out to get a breath of fresh air and find me standing there.

How long should I wait? Would Nell be able to come? Would she even want to? Could she escape a second time without her uncle or aunt knowing? Was I wasting my time, as Charlie'd said?

Maybe I should have been out looking for Owen myself instead of hiding in the shadows near the discarded barrels at the back of the Mansion House. I paced back and forth in the small space, unable to keep still. Daylight was beginning to fade. So little time left to find Owen.

Wherever he was, he'd soon be caught in the darkness for another long, cold night. April nights were not killers like those in January, but they were still close to freezing. Without food or water, wherever he was, Owen had to be in trouble. Deep trouble. If he'd been able to come home by now, he would have.

I focused on the town. On the land. Not on the river beyond Water Street.

Focused so hard I hardly heard the kitchen door open.

Chapter 33

Nell's white dress and fair hair were covered by a dark cloak. She hesitated a moment, and then saw me.

"You came," I said, amazed she'd gotten away.

"You needed my help," she said. "Quickly—we need to leave here before they find I'm not in my room. I told my uncle I had a headache and had to rest."

"Follow me."

The encroaching dusk and Nell's dark cloak helped to hide her identity as we dodged through the alley in back of the Main Street stores, down toward the river, and then toward the *Herald* office. It was the only place I could think of where we could talk.

She stepped inside and looked around. "How wonderful! You have a real printing establishment here." She touched the press and looked at the trays of type Charlie and I'd left unfinished. "What are you working on?"

"I've been asked to print copies of Maine's Act to Raise Volunteers for all the towns in Lincoln County. If I finish the job by Monday morning, I'll be able to pay off what I owe, and I'll own everything here, free and clear. If I don't, then I'll lose the business." I blurted out what I hadn't even told Ma and Pa. Somehow I felt I could tell Nell.

"But instead, you're looking for your friend."

"I couldn't stay here and work when Owen was missing."

"Tell me about him."

161

"Like my letter said, his name is Owen Bascomb and he's nine years old. You answered a question for his parents at your meeting last Saturday. You told them they would have another child."

Nell sat in the chair by the desk. Her expression drifted a little, as it had at the meeting. "I remember."

"They had another son, a boy younger than Owen, but he died of fever. Owen's father tried to enlist yesterday morning, but was told the army didn't want him because he wasn't white. Owen was upset, and ran away."

"Tell me more about Owen. Owen himself." Nell's voice was calm.

"He has a parrot named Gilthead that his uncle, a blue-water mariner, gave him. He works with me here at the print shop. He'd sooner do that than go to school, but he's sharp. He attends classes off and on, and catches up with his lessons quick enough. He doesn't have any close friends his own age that I know of. He brags sometimes, about workin' here. And he bragged about how good a soldier his father would be. Other boys don't like his talkin' as though he's better than they are."

What else was there to say about Owen?

"He's a good boy. A hard worker." I paused. "He's my friend."

Nell didn't say anything. She sat, staring at nothing. Then she began to sway slightly, back and forth, from side to side. "Waters . . . waters . . . separating . . ."

My hands went cold. Owen had drowned, then. Like Ethan. That must be what she was seeing. He was separated from us by the waters. Why had I asked her to help? I didn't want to hear this.

"Soldiers . . . many soldiers. I see soldiers over the water. And gray stones. Lines of gray stones . . ."

Nell stopped. Her voice changed. "That's all; it's gone. But I saw something. It was all mixed up. I don't know this area, or Owen. You'll have to help put the pieces together, Joe."

"Is Owen dead, then?"

"I didn't see that," she said, surprised. "I didn't see him at all, to be truthful. But what I saw had something to do with where he is. Clues."

"You said *waters*. The Sheepscot is deep and wide, and borders Wiscasset. For sure that's the biggest water near here."

"What else did I say?"

"You don't know?"

"When I'm in one of my trances, as I was a few minutes ago, it's a little like being in a dream. I can't always remember what happened." Nell smiled and shrugged. "I'm used to it, but I know it sounds strange. If you need my help, then I need yours to help interpret what I saw and said."

"You said *separating*."

Nell nodded. "That was close to *waters?*"

"Yes, I think so." This was harder than I'd thought it would be. I'd imagined she'd just be able to close her eyes and tell me where Owen was, and I could go and get him. I should have written down everything she'd said.

"The Sheepscot River is right there," Nell said, pointing at the river, which we could now barely see in the darkness through the window. "What does it separate? What's on the other side of the river?"

"That's Davis Island. Part of the town of Edgecomb."

"I remember," Nell said. "You told me that the night we met on the street. I'd wanted to walk on the bridge, and you said it would be too dangerous because of the ice."

"You think Owen might have gone over the bridge to Edgecomb?" I'd never thought of Owen leaving this side of the river. So far as I knew, no one else had thought of that either.

"The other words I said—what were they?"

"*Soldiers. Lines of gray stones.*"

"Is there a graveyard for war veterans in Edgecomb?" Nell asked.

"No," I said, jumping up and grabbing her hand to pull her with me. "Not a graveyard. But I think I know where Owen is now! Thank you!"

I didn't know for sure if Nell was right, but her clue had given me the best idea so far as to where to look for Owen. Maybe those spirits of hers really did know what was happening. If I found Owen, then Charlie'd be proved wrong. Nell wasn't a fraud.

I started toward the door, then stopped. "You should go back to the inn before your uncle finds out you're gone."

"I'm not going back; I'm going with you," said Nell, pulling her cloak around her body. "I've never had an adventure like this. I don't care what my uncle says; if your friend Owen's in trouble, it might be good if there are two of us."

I nodded. I picked up the tin lantern I'd thought to fill at home that morning, and lit it to help guide our way. I hoped it held enough oil to see us there and back.

Most folks in Wiscasset were sitting down to warm suppers as Nell and I started across the Long Bridge toward Edgecomb, and, we hoped, toward Owen. I'd told Ma I'd probably be working late, with the bill from Augusta to print, so she'd think I was either at the office or looking for Owen. What Nell's aunt and uncle would think when they discovered her absence, I couldn't be sure. I just knew it wouldn't be good.

Chapter 34

Our footsteps on the wooden bridge sounded thunderous.

No one else was crossing at this time of night. It felt as though Nell and I were the only two people in the universe. The stars spread above us like embroidery on Ma's best linen tablecloth. Behind us only a few flickering lamps shone bright enough in Wiscasset windows to prove the town was still there.

The dark river murmured below us, and we could hear the slap of the incoming tide hitting the rocks on the shores and the ships moored in the harbor.

"How much of that long document have you finished printing?" Nell asked. I held the lantern slightly in front of us, so we wouldn't trip on the uneven boards of the bridge.

"None," I admitted. "Charlie and I had just started setting the type for the first two pages yesterday, when we heard about Owen."

"How many pages will there be?"

"Ten, I think. Setting the type for each page takes several hours, and then we have to print each page." I might as well admit the truth. "The next edition of the *Herald* is due out Saturday, so I'd hoped to have several pages of the Act in the paper, and then print the rest on Sunday, so it would be ready for the county clerk by Monday morning. I don't think there'll be time now."

"It must be hard to run a business."

"I've always dreamed of publishing a newspaper. But now that Pa's enlisted, Ma will need me at our family's store while he's gone. It would have been hard to keep the paper going and help out at the store, anyway. Maybe it's for the best if I have to give up the paper." I said the words out loud, and tried hard to believe them.

At the end of the bridge we turned right, down a rutted dirt road.

"Where are we going?" Nell asked. "You haven't told me."

"At the end of this road there's an old fort," I explained. "It was built for the War of 1812, to defend Wiscasset from the British. Since then moss and grasses have grown over the fortifications. But you said *many soldiers,* and there were many soldiers at the fort—Americans and, after they were captured, British. And you said *gray stones.* The fortifications were built of granite from the quarry in Edgecomb, so they're gray. It all fits."

Nell stumbled, and I grabbed her elbow.

"I'm fine," she said. "I'm used to cobblestones and plank roads, but roads of hardened mud are hard to navigate in the dark."

I tried to hold the lantern so it was easier for her to see. Her wide, long skirts and cloak were cumbersome. Maybe I shouldn't have let her come.

"How far do we have to go? I'm feeling that Owen needs us," she said suddenly, and started walking faster.

"Perhaps a quarter-mile," I said, smiling to myself. Miss Nell Gramercy might look delicate, but I didn't know any girls in town who'd go for a walk in the dark with someone of the opposite sex, to a place they'd never been.

She looked at me. "I think we should run, if you think the lantern will stay lit." And she took off.

She had to hold up her long hoop skirts and cloak, and though we wouldn't have won any races, we did speed up considerably. We were both huffing and puffing when we made it up the hill at the end of the island where the fort stood, surrounded on three sides by the river, and partially illuminated by the half-moon.

"Owen!" I called out while Nell caught her breath. "Owen! Are you here?"

I walked first to the Wiscasset side of the island, and then to the end. Nell had dropped back and was close to the fort itself.

I'd started down to where the fortifications had been built close to the river when I thought I heard a voice.

"Joe?" Then a pause. "Joe? Is that you?"

"Owen! Where are you?"

"Down here. Near the river. I'm hurt."

"Nell—he's here!" I called up to her, and scrambled down one of the old paths soldiers had worn in the dirt sixty years ago, when taking their positions at the walls. "Owen! Say something!"

"Joe, I fell. My leg's hurt bad. And I'm so cold."

Chapter 35

Thursday, April 18, before midnight

Owen was shivering badly. He'd slipped while making his way down one of the narrow, overgrown trails that wove through the fort's grounds. He had fallen, hitting several of the large granite rocks, and landed on his left leg, which was folded under him at an unnatural angle.

His eyes opened wide as he saw Nell beside me. She knelt on the cold ground and felt his forehead. "He's feverish. We should have thought to at least bring some water with us."

She turned to Owen and spoke softly. "Are you bleeding any-where?"

He shook his head. "Not anymore. Scratches."

"Good." She looked at Owen's leg, but didn't touch it. Then she took off her heavy cape and covered him with it. Her white dress glimmered in the glow of the lantern.

"Joe, we can't move him; his leg is badly broken. We could make it worse. We need to get a doctor with a wagon. You're faster than I am, and you know where to go. I'll stay with Owen and talk with him and keep him warm."

I got up. "How do you know so much about doctoring?"

Nell hesitated. "I had brothers and sisters. I took care of them. You go, now—bring back a doctor."

I started to hand Nell the lantern, but she refused it. "You'll need it to make better time on the road. You don't want to fall and break your own leg. Now, go!"

I left her sitting next to Owen, her arm around him. I think she was singing him a song.

I hardly remember the next hour. Somehow I got back to Wiscasset and told Dr. Cushman. While he was harnessing up his horse and putting water and blankets and lanterns in his wagon, I went to tell the Bascombs.

Mrs. Bascomb loaded more blankets into her husband's arms and hugged and kissed me about ten times, until I was finally able to drag her husband out of there. We ran back to Dr. Cushman's house, where he'd readied his wagon.

I wished I'd had time to let Ma and Pa know what was happening, but everything was happening too fast for such delays. Dr. Cushman did look at me questioningly when I told him that Nell Gramercy was with Owen, but he, too, focused on what had to be done. Questions could be asked and answered later.

The ride back to Fort Edgecomb went quickly. Before I knew it I was leading the doctor and Mr. Bascomb down the uneven path between the rocks where Nell and Owen were.

By now Nell was also shivering, and I could tell something was wrong with her as well, but Owen was so glad to see his father, there was no time for anything but trying not to hurt him too much. We lifted him onto the plank Dr. Cushman had brought, and carried him to the wagon.

Dr. Cushman gave him some medicine for pain, and Owen was brave. I think he was almost too tired to cry or scream. Almost, but not quite. The wagon bumping up and down on the rocky road didn't help. I tried not to look at his face; I figgered he wouldn't want me to see him cry. But the way his leg looked, there wasn't a grown man in Wiscasset who wouldn't have shouted to high heaven and let loose with language the reverend wouldn't have looked on lightly.

Dr. Cushman covered Owen with the blankets he'd brought, and Nell curled up in another corner of the wagon on her cloak.

"What's wrong?" I asked her softly.

"My head," she answered. "It started a while after you'd left. It's pounding. I can hardly see. The jouncing of the wagon makes it worse."

I didn't know what to do. "Do you want us to take you back to the inn?" I asked.

"*No*," she managed to say. "No—please. Don't make me go back there. Let me stay, and see how Owen is. Maybe the doctor can help me, too."

I left her alone, and waited to see what would happen.

About that time I looked up at the sky and realized it must be considerably after midnight. No doubt Nell's aunt and uncle knew she was missing by now.

Owen was safe—but how much trouble was Nell in?

Chapter 36

Friday, April 19, early morning

Dr. Cushman's wife took one look at Nell and brought her to their parlor to lie down.

Mr. Bascomb, Dr. Cushman, and I lifted the plank Owen was on off the wagon and carried it into the doctor's office, where we laid him on a long pine table in the middle of the room. Owen's face, which I could just see under the blankets we'd piled on top of him, was chalky, and the medicine the doctor had given him was beginning to wear off. I hoped he wouldn't think too much about the stuffed birds hanging on the walls around the office.

Dr. Cushman took one of the knives from an assortment of saws and blades on a side table and cut off the right leg of Owen's trousers. Owen winced as the blue wool pulled away from where his bone had broken through the skin. Now-clotted blood had stiffened the material and attached it to his muscle and skin.

Dr. Cushman put a white tablet in Owen's mouth. "Swallow this; it'll make the pain easier to bear." He took a basin of water and washed the grit and dirt and blood off Owen's leg. Then he looked at Mr. Bascomb and me.

"Are you both steady enough to hold the boy while I set this bone? We'll give him a few minutes for the opium to work, but then I'll need to manipulate the bone and put it back inside. If either of you aren't able to do this, tell me now. My wife's helped me before. I can get her."

I didn't want to be there. But I also didn't want to be replaced by Dr. Cushman's wife. I glanced at Mr. Bascomb. He was just looking at Owen, holding his hand.

"I can do it, sir," I said.

Mr. Bascomb nodded. "Go ahead. Get it over with."

The tablet must have been strong. Owen appeared as though he didn't see us—as though he was falling asleep.

"Hold the boy straight, then," said Dr. Cushman. "Bascomb, you hold his head and shoulders, and don't let him move. Joe, put one hand on his right hip and the other on his right knee, and hold them down. Don't let them move. I'll do this as quickly as I can."

The doctor rolled up his sleeves, and before we knew it he'd taken hold of the bone sticking out of Owen's leg and started pushing it back in, pulling the skin right over it.

I watched for a moment, and then couldn't look anymore. I concentrated on holding Owen down. His body under my hands got tighter and tighter. I felt it strain and try to move. I pushed down harder, as though I were pushing, pushing him down through the table. I couldn't see or feel anything except that table and my hands. I didn't even think about Owen. Just about keeping my hands down, and still.

I can't tell you how long it all lasted. It seemed an hour. Probably it was five or six minutes.

Finally Dr. Cushman's voice said, "You can let go. It's done."

I stepped back. Owen's bone was hidden. An angry jagged tear in the skin marked where the bone had been.

"Is he going to be all right?" asked Mr. Bascomb.

"I hope so," said Dr. Cushman. "Unless infection sets in; that's the biggest danger." He was wrapping the wounded leg in clean bandages. Owen lay quietly.

"I'll put a splint on him now; he'll sleep for an hour or two. In the morning we'll take him home in the wagon. Make sure he rests for a couple of days, and then he can walk, using a crutch. If the leg gets red or swells up, let me know immediately. We might have to amputate. The break was clean, but since it broke through the skin, and he was outside for so long, there's danger of gangrene. Only time will tell."

Amputate! I looked down at Owen, as Dr. Cushman bound two small boards around his leg, one on each side, to hold the break together.

"I'll give you a few of the opium pills to use later, when he's home. He can have one every four hours for the first three days, for pain. After that I'll stop in to see how he's doing," Dr. Cushman said to Mr. Bascomb. "There's nothing more we can do for him now. Why don't you go home and tell your wife how he is? Mrs. Cushman and I will take good care of him until you get back."

"Thank you, Doctor," said Mr. Bascomb. "My wife will be waiting for news. I'll be back in a couple of hours. Thank you for everything you've done for my boy."

He bent down and gently put his hand on Owen's forehead. Then he left.

"Now, Joe," said Dr. Cushman, "let's go see about that young lady you brought with you."

Chapter 37

Nell was lying on a sofa in the Cushmans' parlor. She was shaking even though Mrs. Cushman had covered her with quilts. A cloth covered her forehead and eyes, and a hot cup of tea was on the table next to her.

"Miss Gramercy?" asked Dr. Cushman. "How are you feeling?"

"It's only one of my headaches," Nell answered softly. "Your wife has been very kind, but the pain sometimes lasts for hours. Please, could I have some laudanum? That would help."

"Indeed," answered the doctor. "May I see your eyes?" Nell took the cloth off her face and opened her eyes. The doctor looked into them carefully. Then, to my surprise, he picked up her hand and looked at her fingernails. "How long has it been since you had a dose of laudanum?" he asked.

"Not since yesterday morning, I think," she said. "My uncle gives it to me when the headaches come, but they keep getting worse. I take it most days, especially before I have spiritual sessions. It takes the pain away for a while, and makes it easier for me to hear my voices. But then the headaches come back. Don't you have any?"

"My dear girl, you mustn't take any more of that drug. Laudanum is powdered opium mixed with alcohol. It can take the pain away for a while, but should only be used by adults, in extreme and limited circumstances."

Uncertain Glory

Dr. Bascomb looked over at his wife. "I'm seriously concerned about this young woman. I've been reading in medical journals from Europe about the dangerously addictive properties of opium. She's showing all the signs."

He turned back to Nell. "Miss Gramercy . . ."

"Please, call me Nell. I'm only twelve. I get so tired of being Miss Gramercy."

"Then, Nell . . . the laudanum is hurting your body in ways that are hard to even guess at, since you're so young. True, it will take away your pain for a few hours, but it will also destroy your life, if you continue taking it the way you have been."

"But I can't work when my headaches hurt so much."

"Then you must stop working," Dr. Cushman said. "The amount of laudanum you're taking is actually causing the headaches. You get them when you've gone too long without the drug. The only way to totally stop your pain is to stop taking the laudanum."

Nell started to cry.

"Nell," I said, going over and sitting on the floor next to her. "What's wrong? Is it your uncle?"

She nodded through her tears. "I can't stop working. He won't let me stop. My sessions support him and my aunt."

"What about your parents, dear? Haven't you got any other family you could live with?" Mrs. Cushman asked.

Nell shook her head. "My father died when I was little. My older brother drowned, and then Mother and my other brothers and sisters died of consumption. All of them. I was the only one left. I was going to live in the poorhouse until my uncle found out that I sometimes

178

heard voices. He said as long as I heard voices, I had a home with him. He won't let me stop touring. Not ever. I've begged him to let me, but he refuses to listen. And I have nowhere else to go."

"That's criminal," said Dr. Cushman softly. "Parents and guardians have the right to raise a child as they see fit, but only within the bounds of reason and humanity. Drugging a child is a form of abuse. I wonder what Sheriff Chadbourne would say to this—a girl addicted to laudanum and forced to work against her will."

"Would you like to stay in Wiscasset?" I asked suddenly. I hadn't thought it through, but it made sense. "Pa's enlisting, and with Ethan gone, it's just Ma and me. Ma's always said she wanted a daughter. We have room. You could stay with us."

Everyone looked at me.

"Are you sure, Joe?" asked Dr. Cushman.

Pa said I was to be the man of the house when he was gone. I'd just made a major decision. "I'm sure."

"I'm guessing your uncle and aunt don't know where you are, Nell. Am I right?" said Dr. Cushman.

Nell nodded. "I sneaked out of the Mansion House late yesterday afternoon to help find Owen. My aunt and uncle would never have given me permission to leave."

"Do you want to stay here, with Joe's family?" Dr. Cushman looked at her seriously. "Do you want to leave your uncle and aunt and never see them again?"

Nell looked at me. Then she reached her hand out for Dr. Cushman's. "Oh, yes. If that were possible, that's what I would choose."

Dr. Cushman nodded, as though he'd just made a decision, too. "Then I suggest we get you away from here as soon as we can. Dear," he said, turning to his wife, "would you watch over Owen Bascomb while I go and pay a call on Sheriff Chadbourne and apprise him of this situation? In the meantime, Joe, you take Miss Gramercy to your home. Keep her out of sight until the sheriff or I let you know what's to happen."

He smiled at both of us as I helped Nell to her feet. "And I suggest both of you try to get a little sleep. It's been a long night for all of us."

The sun was beginning to come up over the Sheepscot as I showed Nell the long way to my house, down High Street and over to Fore Street and around, on the chance her uncle was out looking for her. We figured he'd be looking on Main Street, or Water Street, or some other section of town more centrally located.

Had Mr. Allen alerted the sheriff himself when he realized Nell was missing? Had he been searching the town for her, just as the townspeople had for Owen? Or had he kept her disappearance a secret, knowing that it could mean the end of her good reputation? Or perhaps, thinking she'd been abducted, as sometimes happened with wealthy children, he'd been waiting for a ransom note. Who knew what he'd been thinking?

All Nell and I wanted was to get to my house as quickly as we could. We slipped in through the kitchen door and were greeted by Trusty, whose barks would have wakened any neighbors not yet up. Ma and Pa were sitting at the kitchen table, where I suspected they'd been all night.

I was so relieved to be home I hardly had time to be nervous.

Ma rushed over and gave me a big hug. "Thank goodness you're home!" she said. After hesitating a moment, she hugged Nell, too. "And you've brought Miss Gramercy with you, too. What a surprise! You both look in need of a hot breakfast."

Nell smiled.

"Nell has a headache," I started.

"It's a little better now, thank you," Nell said softly. "I'd love a cup of tea, please, Mrs. Wood, if it's no trouble."

"Of course, of course," said Ma, bustling about. "And coffee for you, Joe, and your pa."

"What about Owen?" said Pa. "Has anyone found him?"

"We did," I answered as I sat down at the table. To my surprise, despite her headache, Nell helped Ma get cups out of the cabinet.

"Nell's voices knew where to look. We found Owen at Fort Edgecomb. He'd fallen and broken his leg. He's at Dr. Cushman's house right now. His leg is set, and the doctor is hoping he'll be all right. He'll be going home in an hour or two."

"Thank goodness," said Pa. "We were so worried all night. About you, and Owen." He looked over at Nell. "It never occurred to us to be worried about Miss Gramercy as well."

"We're all fine now," said Nell, joining us at the table and handing Pa a cup of coffee. "And, please, call me Nell."

"Pa, Ma, we have something to ask you," I said, looking from one to the other. "Right now Dr. Cushman is seeing Sheriff Chadbourne. You've met Nell's uncle, Mr. Allen. He's been giving Nell dangerous drugs and forcing her to perform those sessions. Dr. Cushman says it's bad for her health, and she needs to stop, but her uncle won't let her. She wants to leave her aunt and uncle, but she has no other family."

Ma and Pa exchanged a look. Ma was the first to speak. She reached out and touched Nell's hand. "I hope you told this dear girl she had a home with us, right here in Wiscasset. We have an extra room in our house, and lots of room in our hearts."

I couldn't help grinning. That was just what I'd thought Ma would say.

Nell started crying. Not sobbing this time—happy tears.

"Thank you so much," she said. "I'd be glad to help you with your store, Mrs. Wood. And I know how to do some cooking, but I'd like to learn more."

"I had two boys, and I've loved 'em both, but I've always wanted a daughter, too. I know it's probably too soon, my dear, but I wouldn't mind if someday, you might stop calling me 'Mrs. Wood' and call me 'Ma,' as Joe does. Or 'Ma Wood,' if you'd like. It'd feel more friendly-like."

Pa smiled, a little crookedly. "I can see my family's changing by the day around here. And for the best. Welcome, Nell. You'll be good company for my wife Catherine and for Joe while I'm away, and having a son and a daughter's not a bad thing at all."

"I have one question for you, though, Nell," I said. "If you're feeling well enough to answer it." I just had to ask her.

"What is it, Joe?"

I swallowed hard. "You say you hear voices, and for sure, you know things no regular person should be able to know. But Charlie and I talked to that bearded man who asked the first question at the assembly you held last week. He said your uncle had paid him to say those things about his having a sweetheart."

Ma and Pa exchanged glances. I hoped they wouldn't be too upset with me for questioning Nell. They truly believed that everything she'd said came from her spirit voices. But before she became part of our family, I wanted to know for sure.

The kitchen was silent. Then Nell said, quietly, "I used to tell people the truth—that the spirits don't always talk to me. But my uncle didn't accept that. He said the spirits must speak to me when people pay for a session. When I first started having large sessions, he planned it out so it would look as though I hadn't heard the questions asked. He said it would seem more mystical."

"So it was a trick? But how did you do it?"

"I hated fooling people . . . but it worked. My uncle would find someone, like the bearded man you talked to, who I would meet beforehand. We would prepare his question and answer in advance. At the session, the first thing I did would be to give out that 'answer.' Then, as you saw, I would pick up a piece of paper with a question on it. But what was on the paper was *not* the question I would read out loud; instead, I would say the first person's prepared question, while reading the written one to myself. After I read it, I'd be able to answer it—sometimes with help from my spirits, sometimes because I could just sense what the writer wanted to hear. So I always saw the question before I gave the answer." She looked down. "I know it was wrong, but it was part of the show."

"It worked really well," I said. So Charlie had been right. Nell *had* tricked people. "So your voices aren't real?"

Ma spoke up. "Joe, leave this poor girl alone. She told you; sometimes she hears voices, but just not all the time. I know for certain what she heard for your pa and me came right from your brother. It had to. That was no trick." She turned to Nell. "Seems to me the problem was your uncle, not letting you answer in your own time. He forced you to pretend when the voices didn't come to you."

Nell nodded. "That's how it was. Thank you for understanding."

"When you live in this house, no one's going to ask you questions. You'll be who you are. If your voices want to tell you something, that'll be between them and you. You shan't be asked to perform."

Nell smiled. "Thank you. You sound a lot like my mother."

"Well, for right now, that's who I'll try to be. And I say that you and Joe had both better get some rest; you've been up the full night. Joe, show Nell where Ethan used to sleep. It'll be her place from now on."

I beckoned to Nell and we headed up the stairs. It had all gone even easier than I'd thought.

Now if it would just go as smoothly with Mr. Allen.

Chapter 38

"Joe! Nell! Come downstairs!"

Ma's excited voice woke me from the heavy sleep I'd fallen into. I shook my head and pulled on my boots. I hadn't even taken off my clothes from the night before; I'd been too tired.

I hoped Nell had been able to sleep, too. But as I clattered down the stairs I saw she'd reached the kitchen before I had. And the room was crowded.

Sheriff Chadbourne, a big man any way you might define that word, filled the space by himself. He was smiling.

"Wanted to check that you folks were all right, and safe here at home. Knew you'd be interested in what happened this morning after Dr. Cushman came to talk with me."

He turned to Nell. "I went and had a little visit with your aunt and uncle, Miss Gramercy. I informed them that here in the State of Maine, we don't hold with folks giving medicine to young girls when it's not needed, and a doctor was willing to testify to such. I also informed them that the same doctor, and others in the community, were willing to testify that Miss Gramercy did not wish to continue traveling with them. I told them that if they tried to contact her again, they would be arrested."

"What did they say to that?" I asked.

"They weren't happy about it, you can be sure. But I told them that if they didn't leave town today, I'd file official abuse and harassment charges and arrest the both of them. Said that in Wiscasset, we don't countenance people taking advantage of children, and my next stop would be Judge Fales's office."

Nell smiled at him. "Thank you, sir."

"Then I waited while your aunt packed up your clothes and such in your trunk," he said, pointing at an elegant leather trunk in the corner of the kitchen. "I thought a young lady would need her personal things."

"Yes, sir!" said Nell. This time her smile was almost as big as Ma's.

"Deputy Hubbard is with your aunt and uncle now, and will be accompanying them this afternoon when they leave on the Boston stage. I've instructed him to remain with them as far as Portland, and then to see them off on the next part of their journey south. He'll alert the driver that if they depart the stage at any town north of Boston, he's to notify law enforcement."

"Thank you so much, Sheriff Chadbourne," Pa said. "Miss Gramercy—Nell—is safe with us. We appreciate all of your help."

"Happy to help out," said Chadbourne, tipping his hat to everyone. "And may I suggest that Miss Gramercy not show her face on Main Street until after the stage has left at one-thirty today."

Sheriff Chadbourne had barely left when the kitchen door banged open and Charlie barged in. For a moment he just stood, looking in amazement at Nell, her trunk, and Ma and Pa and me.

"I heard this crazy story," he said. "That Joe and Nell Gramercy had found Owen at Fort Edgecomb in the middle of the night."

"You heard right," said Pa. "Owen's probably to home by now, healing his broken leg."

"But you haven't even heard the most exciting part," I said. "Nell's aunt and uncle are leaving town, and she's staying here. With Ma and Pa and me."

For a moment Charlie didn't say anything. He looked dumbstruck.

"Godfrey mighty," he managed to say. "That's fierce!" He looked from one of us to the other. Then he got his voice back. "I have news, too. I've enlisted!"

"What?" Even Pa turned around for that. "Charlie, you're not eighteen."

"I'm tall for being close to sixteen. And I got my father to sign a paper saying I just turned eighteen. Edwin Smith accepted me. He needs everybody he can to muster one hundred men for Wiscasset. So I'm going!" Charlie pretended to hold a rifle and pointed it at each of us in the kitchen. "*Pow, pow, pow!* I'm going to get those Confederates! I'm going to be a hero! Just wait and see!"

I couldn't believe Charlie, my friend, was really leaving Wiscasset and going to be a soldier in the army. Charlie, who had trouble keeping his mind on his work, would learn to shoot a gun and fight in battles.

"Captain Smith says we're leaving next Tuesday, the twenty-third. I can help you with your printing until then, Joe. Are you going to work today?"

Tuesday. Pa and Charlie and all the enlisted men would be leaving for the war next Tuesday. Monday was the twenty-second, the day the money was due. Today was Friday.

I only had until Monday morning to get the rest of the money for Mr. Shuttersworth. Three days.

"I'm going now. I can use all the help I can get."

"I'll go with you. I don't know anything about setting type, but maybe I can help with the press," said Nell, smiling. "You've changed my life. Maybe I can help you with yours."

"Go on, the three of you, then," said Ma. "Go the back way, in case Nell's uncle is still wandering about. I'll bring you all some food later. With everything else that's happening, now's the time to focus on the *Herald*."

Only the day before I'd thought it would be impossible.

"I don't know if we can print the Act in time," I said. "But if you're both willing to help . . . let's go!"

WISGASSET HERALD

POST OFFICE BUILDING, SECOND STORY,
WATER STREET, WISCASSET, ME.

CALL FOR VOLUNTEERS!

PRESIDENT Abraham Lincoln has issued a proclamation calling upon the states of the Union to contribute a total of 75,000 volunteers from their various militias in order to suppress the Southern insurrection and defend the United States and its right to exist as a nation. To that end he has requested that citizens volunteer for a period of three months, at which time said militias will be dispersed.

The president also set an extra session of Congress to be held July 4.

Men throughout the North, West, and East of our nation rejoiced that the rebellion would soon be put down and resolved to defend the United States. New York City businesses predicted that the nation's economy would benefit from the stimulation of civil war.

To this date no response to the president's proclamation has come from the slave-owning Border States.

GOD SAVE THE UNION AND CONFOUND ITS ENEMIES

Chapter 39

Tuesday, April 23, midday

My eyes were still burning from lack of sleep, but we'd done it.

Somehow Nell and Charlie and I had set the type and printed the Act and gotten twenty-five copies to the county clerk first thing Monday morning—just in time to collect the money I needed to pay Mr. Shuttersworth his $65. I was even able to give Charlie $6 to take with him soldiering.

While I'd spent most of the weekend at the *Herald* office, Ma'd been busy at the store, helping families to provision their men for the journey, and giving Pa numerous last hugs in preparation for his departure. Her eyes were swollen and red, but so were those of most women, and a few men, in town.

Reverend Merrill began the morning with a special church service to honor those departing to serve our country. He'd even composed a special patriotic hymn which the choir sang in their honor. Then the eighty-nine men (not quite the one hundred Edwin Smith had hoped for) who'd enlisted marched down the Village Green from the church onto Main Street. The entire town lined the block, waving flags and cheering for their family, friends, and neighbors.

Nell and Ma and I stood together near the corner of Water Street, where we could see everything. Right at the corner of Long Bridge and Water Street, Reverend Merrill said another prayer for the soldiers, and Captain Tucker declaimed some fine words about patriotism.

I can't remember just what was said, since most folks were crying, including many of the new soldiers themselves.

Some soldiers were as young as Charlie, and a few were in their forties, but most men were in their twenties and thirties, leaving sweethearts or wives and young children behind. As they marched over the Long Bridge to Edgecomb, the whole town followed them. On the Edgecomb side they were met by the Newcastle town band, which led everyone in a new assortment of hymns and patriotic songs before leading the soldiers up the hill toward Newcastle, their next destination. It would take several days for them to reach their first training ground at Rockland.

As we walked back across the bridge, Ma comforted a young woman whose husband had just left. Nell and I walked together, neither of us saying much.

We'd just gotten back to Main Street when Owen hobbled up on his new crutches. "News! I have news!" he shouted.

"What news?" I asked, trying to smile through the sadness of the day.

"I knew you were busy, so I checked with Miss Averill at the telegraph office," said Owen. "Remember that regiment from Massachusetts that left for Washington last week—the Sixth Massachusetts?"

I remembered. The Massachusetts regiment that had managed to get organized so quickly, ahead of all the other New England regiments.

"They were on their way to Washington—they took a train to Baltimore—but when they started marching south from there, they were attacked by people on the side of the South. Four soldiers and a dozen people in Baltimore were killed. They're the first to die in action in the war, and on the anniversary of Lexington and Concord, too." Owen took a deep breath.

"That's awful, Owen," I said.

"That's not all," he added. "The first man killed a citizen of my color, Nicholas Biddle. Sumner Needham, a soldier from Norway, Maine, was killed too." He looked at me. "Can we put all that in the newspaper, Joe?"

"Yes, we can, Owen," I said, and I put my arm around his shoulders. "The soldiers have gone, but we on the home front still have a job to do."

Owen and Nell and I headed for the *Herald* office. We needed to print a special edition.

Author's Historical Notes

Some of the major characters in *Uncertain Glory,* and many of the minor ones, were real people who lived in Wiscasset, Maine, during the 1860s.

Teenagers Joe Wood and Charlie Farrar did own a printing business in Wiscasset, and published the *Wiscasset Herald,* a four-page newspaper. I've taken the liberty of moving the time of their business from 1859 to 1861, and of giving full ownership to Joe.

Charlie Farrar enlisted in the Union Army. When he and the others serving under Edwin Smith reached Rockland in 1861, the citizens of Rockland and Thomaston gave each of them a small Bible to keep with them while they were serving their country. Some of those small "Testaments" may be found in homes, libraries, and historical society museums in Maine today.

Charlie didn't stay in the army long. Perhaps war wasn't as glorious as he'd thought it would be. Instead, he settled in Massachusetts, where for many years he ran a printing business during the winters. During the summers he lived in northern Maine, where he captained a steamboat in the Rangeley Lakes region, and wrote guides to hunting, fishing, and hiking in the Maine wilderness and adventure stories for boys. Charlie married, but never had children. He died in 1893.

Joe Wood stayed in Wiscasset. At the beginning of the war he served in the Maine Home Guard under Richard Tucker. He then left for Portland, where he served an apprenticeship at the *Portland Evening Courier.* After attending business school he returned to Wiscasset, and, in 1869, began publishing another, more ambitious, Wiscasset newspaper, the *Seaside Oracle* (1869–76). Joe spent the rest of his life in the newspaper business, publishing newspapers in Skowhegan, Bar Harbor, and Bath, Maine. He married in 1880, and named his children Charles Darwin, Herbert Spencer, and Frances (after his wife). He died in 1923.

The group of volunteers that left Wiscasset under the command of Edwin Smith became part of the Fourth Maine Volunteers, together with units from Searsport, Winterport, Damariscotta, and Belfast: a total of 1,085 men, including a band. They were not disbanded until July of 1864. During that period a total of 1,440 men served in the regiment: 170 were killed, 443 were wounded, 137 died of disease, and 40 men died in Confederate prisons. There is a monument to them at Gettysburg. Captain Smith was killed at the Battle of Fair Oaks (also known as the Battle of Seven Pines) in Virginia, on May 31, 1862. His body was returned to Wiscasset for burial.

Nell Gramercy and Owen Bascomb and their families are fictional, but there were real people like them in New England in 1861. In the mid-nineteenth century, between one and two million Americans believed that the dead do not cease to exist, but become spirits who can communicate with the living through "spiritualists." Dozens, perhaps hundreds, of spiritualists toured the country, advertising their services. Many of them were young women and girls who were thought to be particularly sensitive and finely attuned to the voices of spirits.

Pure opium and its liquid form, laudanum, were commonly used during this period, though reports from Europe were beginning to indicate that addiction could be a serious problem. Despite this, there were no other medications as powerful for pain, and opium was widely used to treat soldiers wounded during the Civil War. Many of them returned from the war addicted to the drug.

In 1861 the Union government took control of all northern telegraph lines for the war effort. During the four years of the war, more than 15,000 miles of telegraph wires (all strung between poles) were used exclusively for military communications. In the field, wagons containing reels of insulated wire and telegraph equipment batteries took the telegraph to the front, where, in the North, the telegraph operator's office was usually a tent near either General Meade or General Grant. More than three hundred telegraph operators were either killed or seriously wounded during the war.

President Lincoln spent hours in the telegraph office at the War Department, waiting for messages from the front and sending back commands. At the beginning of the war, both the North and the South used the usual dots and dashes of Morse Code to send information, but as the war continued, both developed secret messaging systems so their telegrams could not be read by the opposition.

All of the events mentioned in the book, except those related directly to Nell and Owen, did take place in Wiscasset during April or early May of 1861. For those wondering why Charlie, Joe, and Nell did not attend school: As in many other states, although public schools were available (the teachers were often recent graduates), Maine had no compulsory education laws until after the Civil War. It was common for students to attend classes only until they felt they'd learned enough reading and arithmetic to pursue whatever their future profession would be. A few students went on to higher education, but most boys stayed at home to help their fathers, or were apprenticed, and girls learned homemaking skills from their mothers or "went into service" with other families.

Although the causes of the American Civil War can be traced to issues whose seeds were planted decades earlier, the war officially began with the bombardment of Fort Sumter in South Carolina on April 12, 1861, and ended with the surrender of General Lee at Appomattox, Virginia, on April 9, 1865. The four years between those dates were the bloodiest in American history.

By the end of the war, approximately half of the military-aged white men in the North had served in either the army or the navy, as had close to eighty percent of the white men in the South. During the first year of the war, African-American soldiers were not welcomed in the army (they were accepted in the navy), but in the summer of 1862, the Militia Act allowed them to enlist, although only to serve under white officers. By the end of the war, 179,000 African-American men had served in 166 black Union regiments.

Of all men who served, on both sides, 620,000 died; 414,000, or two-thirds, died from diseases contracted because of unsanitary conditions in the field and lack of medical supplies and knowledge.

Every citizen in the country was involved in the war. It was fought in farmyards and cornfields. It took sons and fathers away from families who needed their support. Women, children, and men too old or too disabled to fight took over the jobs of the men who were fighting.

More than 70,000 Maine men were in uniform at some time during the war, not including those who served in the Home Guard; 204 of those men came from the little village of Wiscasset. Maine had the highest percentage of volunteers of any Union state: sixty percent of eligible men aged eighteen to forty-five. Close to 9,400 of those men died; an additional 5,800 were discharged for injury or illness; and more than 600 were listed as "missing in action."

On the home front, the Bates Mills in Lewiston, Maine, advertised for 120 girls and boys, "to work nine hours per day to run their machinery extra time, to supply the government with tent cloth, so much needed by our soldiers in the field."

Not all fighting was in the Southern and middle states. In June of 1863, Confederates seized the *Caleb Cushing,* a Union ship in Portland Harbor, and sailed it out to sea before being caught. (The Confederates were captured, but the *Caleb Cushing* was a total loss.) In 1864, Confederate agents held up a bank in Calais, Maine, but they also were captured.

Concerned by these activities, new fortifications were added to protect Portland Harbor. Fort Knox was built to protect the Penobscot River region; Fort Popham was built at the mouth of the Kennebec River; and Fort Edgecomb (near Wiscasset) and Fort McClary (at the mouth of the Piscataqua River in Kittery) were re-garrisoned. Vice President Hannibal Hamlin, who had enlisted as a private in the Maine Home Guard when the war began in 1861, was called to active duty in 1864, and reported at Fort McClary in July of 1864—the only time a president or vice president of the United States has served in active military duty while in office. (Hamlin served as a cook for six months.)

In Chapter 28 of *Uncertain Glory*, Mr. Bascomb mentions the trial of Nathaniel Gordon. Captain Gordon (1834–62), a Portland, Maine, man, was the only American slave trader to be tried, convicted, and executed for being engaged in the slave trade. He was hung in New York City in 1862.

Bibliography

This list does not begin to fully represent the sources consulted in writing *Uncertain Glory,* but does suggest some resources for anyone interested in information about the Civil War and, particularly, its effect on children and young people in both the North and the South. I have also included several books on the fascinating subject of spiritualism in nineteenth-century American history and culture.

Beattie, Donald, Rodney M. Cole, and Charles G. Waugh (eds.). *A Distant War Comes Home: Maine in the Civil War Era*. Camden, ME: Down East Books, 1996.

Braude, Ann. *Radical Spirits: Spiritualism and Women's Rights in Nineteenth-Century America*. Bloomington: Indiana University Press, 1989 (second edition).

Chambers II, John Whiteclay (ed.). *The Oxford Companion to American Military History*. New York: Oxford University Press, 1999.

Hoar, Jay S. *Callow, Brave and True: A Gospel of Civil War Youth*. Gettysburg, PA: Thomas Publications, 1999.

Marten, James. *The Children's Civil War*. Chapel Hill & London: The University of North Carolina Press, 1998.

Murphy, Jim. *The Boys' War: Confederate and Union Soldiers Talk About the Civil War*. New York: Clarion Books, 1990.

Podmore, Frank. *Mediums of the Nineteenth Century* (volumes 1 and 2). New Hyde Park, NY: University Books, Inc., 1963 (reprint of 1902 book).

Sears, Stephen W., Aaron Sheehan-Dean, and Brooks D. Simpson (eds.). *The Civil War: The First Year Told By Those Who Lived It.* New York: Penguin Group, The Library of America, 2011.

Soodalter, Ron. *Hanging Captain Gordon: The Life and Trial of an American Slave Trader.* New York: Atria Books, 2006.

Stuart, Nancy Rubin. *The Reluctant Spiritualist: The Life of Maggie Fox.* New York: Harcourt, Inc., 2005.

Weisberg, Barbara. *Talking to the Dead: Kate and Maggie Fox and the Rise of Spiritualism.* San Francisco: Harper, 2004.

Williams, David. *A People's History of the Civil War: Struggles for the Meaning of Freedom.* New York: The New Press, 2005.

About the Author

Lea Wait lives on the coast of Maine, where she writes both historical novels for eight- to fourteen-year-olds, and mysteries for adult readers. Lea grew up in Maine and New Jersey, graduated from Chatham College, earned graduate degrees from New York University, and worked for AT&T while she was raising the four daughters she adopted as a single parent. She is now the grandmother of eight and is married to artist Bob Thomas. She invites readers to visit her website (www.leawait.com) for a teachers' guide and discussion questions for *Uncertain Glory,* as well as information about her other books. She welcomes readers of all ages to friend her on Facebook, where she posts frequently about reading, writing, and living in Maine.

Also by Lea Wait

For Children	For Adults
Stopping to Home	*Shadows at the Fair*
Seaward Born	*Shadows on the Coast of Maine*
Wintering Well	*Shadows on the Ivy*
Finest Kind	*Shadows at the Spring Show*
	Shadows of a Down East Summer
	Shadows on a Cape Cod Wedding
	Shadows on a Maine Christmas

POOR
HOUSE

ROUTE 27

ROUTE 1

TO: BATH, WOOLWICH

D

C

H

G

VILLAGE
GREEN

WARREN STREET

WASHINGTON

MIDDLE

B

MAIN STRE

HIGH STREET

LEE STREET

I

BRADBURY ST.

5TH ST. (SUMMER ST.)

L

4TH ST. (PLEASANT ST.)

FT. HILL ST. (GARRISON ST.)

E

MIDDLE STREET

B

MUD FLATS

FORE STREET

JOHNSTON'S

TINKHAMS
SHIPYARD

Wiscasset, Maine
1861